YORK NOT[

General Editors: Professor
of Stirling) & Professor Su[
University of Beirut)

G000162581

Henry James

THE PORTRAIT OF A LADY

Notes by Marshall Walker

MA PH D (GLASGOW)
Lecturer in English and American Literature,
University of Glasgow

LONGMAN
YORK PRESS

YORK PRESS
Immeuble Esseily, Place Riad Solh, Beirut.

LONGMAN GROUP LIMITED
Burnt Mill,
Harlow, Essex

First published 1981
ISBN 0 582 78256 2

Printed in Hong Kong by
Wing Tai Cheung Printing Co. Ltd.

Contents

Part 1

Introduction

Henry James

Henry James was born in New York City on 15 April 1843, one year after his brother, William. Their grandfather had made enough money in business to free his descendants from the need to work for a living. Their father, Henry James Senior, was a cultured man with a keen interest in religion and philosophy. He travelled all over Europe, taking his family with him. The children were educated by private tutors in New York and given special schooling in England, Switzerland, France, and Germany.

The elder Henry James wanted his children to be, above all, aware of people, places, art, and ideas. With this background it is not surprising that both William and Henry James Junior became students of perception. Encouraged by their father to value their own perceptions of the world, they both spent their lives considering the ways in which people see things and how they react to what they see. William became a philosopher and a pioneer of psychology in the United States. Henry turned psychology into art in his fiction.

In 1858 the James family returned from Europe to America. Like William, Henry studied painting briefly and entered the famous Law School at Harvard University. He left without taking a degree, and began to write reviews and short stories. In 1875 he went to Paris where he met Turgenev, the Russian novelist, and came under the influence of the great French writers of the period, Flaubert, Maupassant, and Zola. Each of these writers had his own distinctive method and style, but they all believed that the art of fiction was a deeply serious activity whose purpose was to examine the ways in which people live. This became James's belief. The seriousness of his approach to the art of fiction is evident not only in his stories and novels, but also in the many essays he wrote about other writers and about the form and principles of the novel.

In 1877 Henry James settled permanently in England. Most of his works are set in Europe and many of them develop what became known as James's 'international theme', that is, they tell stories about Americans in Europe or, less often, Europeans in America. *The American* (1877) and *Daisy Miller* (1878) are about young Americans who make mistakes in France and Italy. In *Daisy Miller* the mistake is tragic and the heroine dies. The American girl in *The Portrait of a Lady* (1881) comes to wish for death as an escape from the mistake she makes in Europe. Instead of allowing Isabel Archer to die, James increases her awareness of life: as her perceptions become sharper, her consciousness expands.

Henry James's career extended from the end of the American Civil War to the middle of the First World War. His output was vast. In addition to his twenty-two novels, he wrote over a hundred short stories, several volumes of essays, plays, books of travel, biography, autobiography, and thousands of letters. In all this there is no better place to begin than *The Portrait of a Lady*. The novel shows James in full command of his powers, but uses simpler language than later novels such as *The Wings of the Dove* (1902) and *The Ambassadors* (1903) in which he also employs the international theme.

In 1915 Henry James became a British citizen. He was angry with America for hesitating to come to Britain's aid during the First World War, and wished to declare his own feelings for the country he had adopted as his home. He was awarded the British Order of Merit shortly before his death on 28 February 1916.

Henry James and the novel

By the time Henry James began to write his early works, American literature had much to be proud of, especially in the novel. The 'Leather-stocking' novels (1823–41) of James Fenimore Cooper (1789–1851) had created the hunter, Natty Bumppo, whose home was the American wilderness. Nathaniel Hawthorne's (1804–64) stories and novels—*The Scarlet Letter* (1850) chief among them—had dealt with the early Puritan culture of New England. Herman Melville (1819–91) had broken all the rules of fiction in *Moby Dick* (1851), his great epic of Captain Ahab and the white whale.

These books all contain their own vision of life, their own kind of truth, but they have one important thing in common: none of them is realistic. Natty Bumppo is an ideal of freedom; Hawthorne's New England belongs to the imagination; in Ahab and the whale Melville created the most powerful symbols in American literature.

As a young writer, James was encouraged by the American novelist William Dean Howells (1837–1920), best known today for *The Rise of Silas Lapham* (1885). Howells was fascinated not by ideals, allegories, or symbols, but by 'real life', and this became James's passion too.

The writers James met in France were, like Howells, concerned with the real world, but James felt that they sometimes concentrated too much on the surface of life. His own aim was to portray life from the inside. A novel by James is designed to give 'an air of reality' and to be a 'representation of life', but interest is focused on the minds of the characters. It is not photographic but psychological realism that we find in his work.

James uses symbols when they can help him to enlarge his meaning. In *The Portrait of a Lady* different houses symbolise different styles of life. He often makes images function as symbols to convey several meanings simultaneously; but the purpose of his novels is, above all, to explore the ways in which 'real' people see and relate to each other.

The 'international theme'

During his own lifetime this was James's most famous subject—the meeting of America and Europe. Compared to Europe, America was still a new, innocent country. European subtleties of manners and morality, evolved over many centuries, baffled the visiting American who was accustomed to directness of behaviour and simple notions of right and wrong. The heroine of *Daisy Miller* does not understand that she cannot behave in Europe as she does in her home town of Schenectady, New York. Christopher Newman, hero of *The American*, thinks mistakenly that money can buy happiness in Europe as it does in America. In *The Portrait of a Lady* Isabel Archer is determined to be free. She fails because her American background has not prepared her for the evil that traps her in Europe.

An unusual feature of the international theme in *The Portrait of a Lady* is that, apart from two nuns who are minor characters, we do not meet any true Europeans face to face. Early readers of the novel would have expected the innocent American heroine to find herself up against an assortment of sophisticated and corrupt Europeans. Instead, Isabel Archer is deceived by corrupt Americans who live in Italy. James seems to suggest that people like Osmond, the villain, and his accomplice, Madame Merle, are more at home in Europe than in the brave new world of America.

Henry James's method

In the preface to *The American* which he wrote for the 'New York' edition of his novels (1907-9), James describes his method of telling Christopher Newman's story:

> He was to be the lighted figure, the others . . . were to be the obscured; by which I should largely get the effect most to be invoked, that of a generous nature engaged with forces, with difficulties and dangers, that it but half understands.

There are two points to notice here. (1) There would be no doubt that

Newman, the one 'lighted' figure, was the central character of the story. (2) Only Newman's character was to be clearly shown. All other characters would remain to some extent dim, undefined, 'obscured', even to the reader. This would encourage the reader to identify with Newman's difficulty in understanding the strange people he meets in Europe.

This is James's method in *The Portrait of a Lady*. Isabel Archer is the one 'lighted figure' whose character is revealed to us from the beginning. All the other people in the novel are kept more or less 'obscured', mysterious, until we near the conclusion. Like Newman, Isabel possesses a 'generous nature' which is 'engaged with difficulties and dangers that it but half understands'.

In the preface to *The Portrait of a Lady* James says he had invented his heroine some time before he wrote the book. The image of a 'young feminine nature' was a 'treasure' which he wished to 'place right' (p.x), that is, he had a clear idea of Isabel but did not yet know what her story would be. He seemed to wake up one morning with all the ingredients he needed, all the characters who would themselves suggest to his imagination exactly how they would relate to Isabel, thereby creating the plot of the novel (p.xiv). As in *The American*, the focus is on the consciousness of the central figure who first suggested herself to James (p.xiii): the other characters are there to interact with her. Their function is to bring out her nature and provoke her mind to activity so that its qualities are revealed.

A note on the text

The Portrait of a Lady was first published in serial form in *Macmillan's Magazine* (London), XLII–XLV, and *Atlantic Monthly* (New York), XLVI–XLVIII, 1880–1. The first English edition of the book was published in three volumes by Macmillan, London, 1881, the first American edition by the Houghton Mifflin Company, Boston, 1882.

James made extensive revisions of a selection of his works for the 'New York' edition of his *Novels and Tales* (1907–9), twenty-four volumes (two more were added posthumously) with new prefaces, published by Charles Scribner's Sons, New York. *The Portrait of a Lady* occupies Volumes 3 and 4.

The Novels and Stories of Henry James, based on the 'New York' edition, but including work James had omitted from his selection, was edited by Percy Lubbock and published in thirty-five volumes by Macmillan, London, 1921–3. *The Portrait of a Lady* occupies Volumes 6 and 7 of this edition.

These Notes are based on the edition of *The Portrait of a Lady* in the Penguin Modern Classics series, Penguin Books, Harmondsworth, 1963, reprinted 1979. Page references are to this edition.

Part 2

Summaries
of THE PORTRAIT OF A LADY

A general summary

The 'lady' whose portrait is painted in the novel is Isabel Archer, an attractive and intelligent young woman from the town of Albany in the state of New York. Isabel's parents are dead, her sisters married. She is free to accept the invitation of her aunt, Mrs Touchett, to go with her to Europe.

The opening scene of the novel introduces us to Gardencourt, a country house near London where Isabel's uncle, Mr Touchett, his son, Ralph, and their friend, Lord Warburton, are discussing the expected arrival of Mrs Touchett and Isabel. At the beginning of Chapter 2 Isabel arrives. Her uncle and Ralph take an immediate liking to her and she is soon offered a proposal of marriage by Lord Warburton, which she refuses. Isabel is determined to keep her freedom and to see as much of life as possible before she chooses a husband. When an American businessman, Caspar Goodwood, comes to renew his earlier offer of marriage, he, too, is refused. This is much to the annoyance of Isabel's journalist friend, Henrietta Stackpole, who has encouraged Goodwood and believes that Isabel should remain true to her American origins.

At Gardencourt Isabel meets Madame Merle, a friend of Mrs Touchett's who seems a model of freedom and accomplishment.

By this time it is clear that Isabel has made a deep impression on her cousin, Ralph Touchett. Incurably ill, Ralph cannot become one of her suitors. Instead, he persuades the dying Mr Touchett to leave Isabel seventy thousand pounds in his will. (The equivalent in 1980 would approach one million pounds.) When Mr Touchett dies, this money frees Isabel from the limitations of her small income and enables her to explore life as she wishes.

After a short visit to Paris, Isabel goes with her aunt to Florence where Madame Merle introduces her to Gilbert Osmond, a widowed American connoisseur who has settled permanently in Italy and lives alone with his daughter, Pansy.

Both Warburton and Goodwood come to Italy and repeat their declarations of love for Isabel, but she is increasingly attracted by the manners and tastes of Gilbert Osmond.

After a year of travel with Madame Merle, Isabel marries Osmond and they go to live in Rome.

Three years later Isabel's marriage has become a misery to her, although she tries not to show this in public. Osmond, she realises, married her for her money. He is a bully who must have his own way, and it now becomes his ambition to marry Pansy to Lord Warburton. Isabel obediently encourages the marriage, until she realises that Pansy is firm in her loyalty to a young man called Edward Rosier, and that Warburton's love is still for herself.

Ralph sends Isabel word from Gardencourt that he is dying and would like to see her. Osmond opposes her going. Osmond's sister, the Countess Gemini, tells Isabel that Pansy is the illegitimate daughter of Osmond and Madame Merle. Isabel's marriage had been arranged to provide Osmond with money and Pansy with a substitute mother. Shocked, Isabel decides to go to Ralph but promises Pansy that she will return.

Isabel is met in London by Henrietta Stackpole, with whom she spends one night before going to Gardencourt.

At their last meeting Isabel and Ralph recognise their profound love for each other.

Goodwood appears and passionately entreats Isabel to leave Osmond and go away with him, but Isabel refuses once more. She returns to Rome, where Osmond and Pansy await her.

Detailed summaries

Chapter 1

It is summer 1871. The opening scene of the novel is set in the grounds of Gardencourt, an old English country house overlooking the river Thames about forty miles from London. The owner of the house is Mr Daniel Tracy Touchett, an ageing American banker now in poor health. He and his son, Ralph, who suffers from a lung disease, are contrasted with the vigorous and handsome Lord Warburton, an ideal example of the English aristocracy, who has come on horseback to visit them from his own estate nearby. As the three men take afternoon tea together, the Touchetts refer to their visitor's need of a wife. Lord Warburton shows little enthusiasm for marriage, but admits that an 'interesting' woman might have some effect on him.

The conversation turns to Mrs Touchett who is expected to arrive at Gardencourt. She has sent word that she is bringing a niece whom she has 'discovered' in America. Mr Touchett hopes the niece is not coming to England to look for a husband. He warns Lord Warburton not to fall in love with her.

COMMENTARY: The 'sense of leisure' (p.5) given by the unhurried talk over tea underlines the fact that this is a place where time is respected.

Henry James gives an account of the old Tudor house representing it as a symbol of English history. Each reference to the history of the house adds to the peculiarly English quality of the scene that awaits the arrival of James's peculiarly American heroine.

The lady whose portrait will be painted does not appear in this chapter, but the stage is set for her entry. Like the three men at Gardencourt, we, as readers, end this chapter wondering what Mrs Touchett's niece will be like.

NOTES AND GLOSSARY:
Edward the Sixth: King of England (1547–53)
the great Elizabeth: Queen of England (1558–1603)
Cromwell's wars: the English Civil Wars (1642–51), which led to the ascendancy of Oliver Cromwell, Lord Protector of England (1653–8)
telegraph: telegram

Chapter 2

Isabel Archer arrives and is delighted by Gardencourt. When she is introduced to Lord Warburton she exclaims, 'It's just like a novel!' (p.17). Explaining how she comes to be there with her aunt, she is quick to assert her independence and dismisses Ralph's suggestion that Mrs Touchett has 'adopted' her. 'I'm not a candidate for adoption,' she says (p.21).

COMMENTARY: Isabel is impressed by Gardencourt but she is not over-awed. She makes an even greater impression on the three men than they do on her. Mr Touchett finds her delightful, but her impact on Ralph makes him untypically 'awkward' (p.20). Lord Warburton keeps his 'excellent manner' (p.19) but Isabel does provoke him into saying to Ralph that she is his 'idea of an interesting woman' (p.21).

NOTES AND GLOSSARY:
Early Tudor: the Tudor period in English history refers to the years 1485–1603, when the Tudor family occupied the throne of England. Gardencourt cannot have been built before 1547 because of the reference to King Edward VI in Chapter 1. A distinctive style of architecture known as 'Late Perpendicular' is associated with this period

---

Chapter 3

Mrs Touchett lives in Florence, virtually separated from her husband. She usually spends one month of the year in London with him, and makes regular trips to America. On her last trip she had found Isabel reading in the drab old house in Albany. The house was once Isabel's grandmother's and later her father's; but Isabel's parents are both dead and the house is to be sold.

Mrs Touchett was attracted to a young woman forthright enough to call her 'crazy Aunt Lydia' (p.26) and honest enough to admit that she would promise 'almost anything' (p.29) to go to Florence. (The key word here is 'almost'.) This was good enough for Mrs Touchett: she will take her niece to Europe.

COMMENTARY: This chapter establishes the young Isabel's 'romantic' disposition. As a child in the Albany house she never looked behind the green paper that covered the glass sidelights of the office door because she preferred to imagine what might be there rather than see the dull reality of the stoop and the pavement. When her aunt appears, Isabel, no longer a child, is reading a history of German thought to improve her 'vagabond' mind. Both as a fanciful child and as a self-disciplining young woman, Isabel is, above all, independent.

The dreariness of the Albany house and its outlook is in obvious contrast to the beauty of Gardencourt with its fine view of the Thames.

NOTES AND GLOSSARY:

Albany: a small town, but the capital of New York State since 1797

sidelights: small windows at the sides of doors

stoop: small porch, platform or staircase

Chapter 4

This chapter centres on the stimulating but irregular education the Archer girls received from their father and on Isabel's 'immense curiosity about life' (p.35).

She has two sisters. Lilian (Mrs Ludlow) is 'practical' and plain; Edith (Mrs Keyes) is pretty. Isabel is pretty too, but is regarded as the 'intellectual' (p.30). Lilian thinks of her as a 'free greyhound' (p.30)— the independence theme again.

As Isabel sits recalling the past, a servant announces the arrival of Caspar Goodwood, a young suitor. At the end of the chapter it is implied that Mr Goodwood has unsuccessfully proposed to Isabel, but that he will try again.

COMMENTARY: Although Isabel thinks of her past as 'fortunate' and 'happy' (p.33), she is determined to progress from it into a fuller experience of the world, and not be like her sisters, locked in their marriages. So far her imagination has enabled her to live in terms of novels, literary periodicals, music, poetry and grand events remote from her daily life. She longs now to participate in life instead of merely imagining it. She is, of course, likely to find the real world more complicated than anything she has read about. As Mr Touchett says in Chapter 6, 'I believe the novels have a great deal of ability, but I don't suppose they're very accurate' (p.57).

Isabel is to be given her freedom and, like a greyhound, will rush headlong into life. We have been warned that life may wound her, for her innocence makes her vulnerable.

NOTES AND GLOSSARY:

Civil War: the American Civil War (1861–5)

London Spectator: not to be confused with the famous eighteenth-century periodical, this *Spectator* was a weekly publication begun in 1828 as an organ of 'educated radicalism'

Gounod: French composer (1818–93)

Browning: English poet (1812–89)

George Eliot: pen name of Mary Ann Evans, English novelist (1819–80)

Chapter 5

After his education at Harvard University and the University of Oxford, Ralph Touchett travelled for two years before taking a position in his father's bank. Eighteen months later he contracted a disease of the lungs (presumably tuberculosis) and now spends his winters abroad. Ralph accepts that his health restricts him to observing life more than participating in it; he may love, but does not expect to be loved in return.

Mrs Touchett admits to Ralph that she has taken Isabel under her wing because she thinks Isabel will do her 'credit' (p.43), but denies that she wishes to shape Isabel's life. She recognises that Isabel 'will do everything she chooses' (p.44).

Lord Warburton visits Gardencourt but leaves before dinner. Isabel presses Ralph to show her the Touchett art collection. While they look at the pictures she asks him if the house conforms to her romantic idea of such a place by having a ghost. Ralph suggests that the ghost may be seen only by someone who has suffered. Isabel thinks people suffer too easily. She came to Europe 'to be as happy as possible' (p.49).

COMMENTARY: Ralph and Isabel are alike. Isabel, we know, values her independence highly, and Ralph has 'a mind that greatly enjoyed its independence'. The difference between them is emphasised at the end of the chapter. Isabel wants knowledge and happiness; Ralph understands that knowledge (seeing 'the ghost') involves suffering.

Chapter 6

Isabel thinks a great deal about the values of 'beauty, bravery and magnanimity'. She is to be admired for the 'nobleness' of her imagination, but her thoughts tend to be 'vague' and she is too ready to settle for a 'general impression of life'. She is aware that thousands of people are less fortunate than herself, but this does not affect her as much as it should.

She admires Henrietta Stackpole who is paying for her nieces' education out of her earnings as a journalist. Henrietta represents independence: she demonstrates that a woman can stand on her own feet without a man to support her.

The 'rich perfection' of Gardencourt is completely to Isabel's taste. She spends many hours in the company of her uncle. Mr Touchett's wisdom comes not from books but from observation of life: 'I just kept quiet,' he says, 'and took notes.'

COMMENTARY: James shows us the mixture of good and bad in Isabel's character. Her imagination, vitality and curiosity are attractive qualities, but her vagueness and complacency are such obvious faults that James warns the reader not simply to analyse his heroine ('she would be an easy victim of scientific criticism'), but to be 'tender' and 'expectant'. We must preserve our sympathy for Isabel and expect to be impressed by her.

Chapter 7

Mrs Touchett is very anti-British. Isabel defends the British way of life and objects that her aunt has no 'point of view', while her own is 'thoroughly American'. Mrs Touchett retorts that she does have a point of view: it is not American but 'personal'.

While Ralph teases Isabel for being so American, he realises that if he is not in love with his cousin he certainly finds her an intelligent, original and fascinating companion.

One evening Isabel wishes to sit up with Ralph and Lord Warburton after her aunt has gone to bed. Mrs Touchett insists that it is improper for a young girl to sit alone with gentlemen late at night. This is not Albany, but England. Isabel's anger fades and she tells her aunt that she wishes always to be told the right and wrong of a situation so that she may decide for herself.

COMMENTARY: Isabel realises that her aunt's 'personal point of view' is similar to her own way of making judgements. Independence is based on having one's own personal point of view and making decisions for oneself.

NOTES AND GLOSSARY:
'Columbia':   a feminine personification of America, derived from Columbus

Titian: Italian painter (1477–1576); leader of the Venetian School

---

Chapter 8

Lord Warburton invites Isabel to visit his estate, Lockleigh, but his two unmarried sisters will come to see her first. He tells Isabel about his brothers: one is a vicar, the other is in the army in India and 'a horrid Tory' (a man of excessively right-wing views, supporting the Tory or Conservative party in British politics). Warburton thinks of himself as a radical man, eager for change in British society. He tells Isabel that Americans are the most conservative people of all. Mr Touchett admits to being a conservative—he likes things the way they are.

Ralph points out that Warburton is muddled in his thinking: he wishes to change the class system of British society but fails to realise that such a change would, logically, strip him of his own privileges. Isabel imagines a revolution would be delightful, but thinks she would be a 'loyalist' (loyal to the old order) so that she could behave 'picturesquely'. She is amusing herself with the idea of playing a grand heroic role, like an aristocrat going proudly to the guillotine at the time of the French Revolution.

Mr Touchett finally agrees that Warburton is to be pitied. We sense that he says this not because of Warburton's anxiety about British society, but because it looks as if Warburton may be hurt by Isabel.

COMMENTARY: Although Warburton's political opinions are confused, they show that he cares about other people. Isabel likes the idea of a political upheaval because a revolution might give her an opportunity to look noble. Warburton is concerned for his country; Isabel thinks of her own image.

NOTES AND GLOSSARY:
an awful Philistine: a person altogether indifferent to culture
you're a lady, my dear, but I ain't a lord: Mr Touchett makes a pun on 'lady' as the title for a lord's wife and 'lady' as a courteous term for 'woman'
disestablish: change the status. Mr Touchett refers to people, like Lord Warburton, who wish to make British society more democratic by undoing the established system which allocates privilege according to birth or wealth
a seat in Parliament: here, a place in the British House of Lords

Chapter 9

Lord Warburton's sisters visit Isabel to invite her to luncheon, and she goes to Lockleigh with Ralph and Mrs Touchett. Isabel likes the Misses Molyneux. They are friendly but dull, and know very little about their brother's political views. Lockleigh appeals to her romantic imagination because it seems 'like a castle in a legend' (p.78); but her walk with Warburton troubles her. She senses that he is courting her and tells him she will not return to Lockleigh. At the end of the chapter she fears for her freedom.

COMMENTARY: The picture of Warburton's sisters at home, contentedly embroidering, typifies the passive kind of life Isabel does not want. Warburton, therefore, seems to threaten her freedom when he makes it clear that he is attracted to her. Isabel is afraid: she does like Warburton—but she likes her independence more.

NOTES AND GLOSSARY:
in the ancient expanses: in the large rooms of the old house
crewels: wool yarns used in embroidery

Chapter 10

Isabel receives a letter from her journalist friend, Henrietta Stackpole, who has just arrived in London and wishes to be introduced to people of importance, so that she can write about them for the *New York Interviewer*. Ralph and Isabel meet her at the railway station and Henrietta immediately begins to ask questions, some of them very personal. She is rude to Ralph, criticising his lack of employment without considering that there might be a good reason for it. The tolerant Ralph manages to be pleasant to her, but tells Isabel that Henrietta smells 'of the Future—it almost knocks one down!' (p.94).

COMMENTARY: Henrietta has 'no sense of privacy' (p.87), but walks stridently into people's lives 'without knocking at the door' (p.93). Her brashness illustrates what can happen when independence and directness are carried to extremes.

NOTES AND GLOSSARY:
car-conductor: American railway-train attendant
a journal of the other world: an American periodical
Constable: English landscape painter (1776–1837)
Lancret: French painter (1690–1743), best known for humorous pictures of society
you truckle to them: you are submissive to them

Chapter 11

Mrs Touchett dislikes Henrietta's vulgarity. Henrietta dislikes Mrs Touchett's undemocratic reliance on servants.

Henrietta tells Isabel that Caspar Goodwood came to England on the same boat as she did. A letter arrives from Goodwood asking permission to visit Isabel. As Isabel looks up from the letter from her American suitor, she sees her English one, Lord Warburton, standing before her.

COMMENTARY: There is a clear similarity between Henrietta and Isabel, on which Isabel herself remarks towards the end of Chapter 15. When Isabel asks if she is to be married, Henrietta replies, 'Not till I've seen Europe' (p.97). Isabel has already refused Caspar Goodwood, and is aware of the danger of Lord Warburton's attracting her away from her avowed intention to see as much of life as possible.

NOTES AND GLOSSARY:
tenue: (*French*) manner

Chapter 12

Isabel's first impulse is to go indoors where there might be other people, rather than linger in the grounds alone with Warburton. Restraining her, Warburton proposes marriage. He had fallen in love with her 'at first sight, as the novels say' (p.104). This makes Isabel feel like a 'wild, caught creature in a vast cage'(p.108). She knows she cannot accept Warburton's proposal any more than she could accept Goodwood's, but she is anxious not to appear insensitive or ungrateful. Promising Warburton she will write to him, she returns to the house, wondering if her rejection of his proposal means she is becoming cold and hard.

COMMENTARY: Isabel might be the heroine of one of the romantic novels that have shaped her mind: the obscure American girl is sought in marriage by an English lord. We sympathise with the good Warburton, but the real achievement of the chapter is that we sympathise even more with Isabel.

Chapter 13

Isabel discovers that Warburton had already written to her uncle, disclosing his intention to propose to her. Mr Touchett does not try to persuade Isabel to accept Warburton, but he shrewdly suggests that she 'might have to pay too much' (p.114) for what she wants from life.

We are given more information about Caspar Goodwood. After a Harvard education he became interested in machines, invented an improved method of spinning cotton and now manages his family's cotton factory. Isabel finds Goodwood admirable, but his conversation tedious and his dress dull. He is too straightforward and unimaginative for her, and she fears his energy and determination.

Isabel writes to Warburton, refusing his proposal and thanking him. Henrietta prevails on Ralph to invite Goodwood to Gardencourt. She wishes to remind Isabel of American values and is worried that her friend may become attached to a wicked ('fell') European. Goodwood declines the invitation. Henrietta proposes a trip to London and persuades Isabel to accompany her. Ralph decides to go too.

COMMENTARY: Henrietta wants to rescue Isabel from the spell that England seems to have cast on her, and believes that the solid, American Goodwood would be the right husband for her. Isabel is nervous but resolute: she will not be caged.

NOTES AND GLOSSARY:

the Civil strife:	the American Civil War (1861–5)
Caliban, Ariel and Prospero:	characters in *The Tempest* by William Shakespeare. Caliban is a misshapen, brutish creature; Ariel is a spirit; Prospero is a magician
fell:	here, ruthless, cunningly destructive
Dickens:	English novelist (1812–70)
the Abbey:	Westminster Abbey in London
Doctor Johnson:	English man of letters (1709–84)
Goldsmith:	Irish writer (1730–74)
Addison:	English writer (1672–1719)
Covent Garden:	district in London famous for theatres and, until recently, its fruit and vegetable market

Chapter 14

About a week after receiving Isabel's letter, Lord Warburton comes to Gardencourt with his sister. At lunch he sits beside Henrietta who tells him she disapproves of lords and dares him to give up his position. Warburton treats her rudeness with cheerful tolerance.

Warburton tells Isabel he cannot understand why she has refused him. Isabel's answer is that to marry him would be to evade her fate by separating herself from life.

Mrs Touchett asks Isabel why she has told her uncle about Lord Warburton's proposal. Isabel replies that her uncle knows Warburton better than her aunt does. Mrs Touchett says that she knows Isabel better, then proves herself wrong by supposing that her niece has refused Warburton because she expects 'to do something better' (p.136), that is, make a more advantageous marriage.

COMMENTARY: Warburton's kindness and self-control are especially evident in this chapter. Henrietta represents a comic version of the American point of view at its most prejudiced.

Looking at Miss Molyneux, Isabel realises what she is rejecting by not marrying Warburton: 'the peace, the kindness, the honour, the possessions, a deep security and a great exclusion' (p.134). Her fate, however, is not to be separated from the realities of life from which such a marriage would exclude and protect her.

Chapter 15

Ralph escorts Henrietta and Isabel to London. They take rooms at Pratt's Hotel while he stays at his father's London house in Winchester Square. Isabel is fascinated by the sights of London but Henrietta wants to meet 'the leading minds of the present' (p.140) and is impatient with places of historical interest. Ralph introduces Henrietta to his friend, Mr Bantling, an energetic, amiable man.

When Henrietta goes to dine with American friends, Ralph asks Isabel why she has refused Warburton. Isabel replies that like Henrietta, she does not wish to marry until she has seen Europe. Ralph wonders if Isabel wants 'to see, but not to feel' (p.150), but Isabel says that this distinction cannot be made about a truly conscious ('sentient') person.

COMMENTARY: Ralph's main interest in life is watching Isabel. She is the 'goose' whose eggs supply him with 'inimitable omelettes' (p.149), the unique food that keeps him alive. If his health were good he would surely permit himself to be in love with her (as he almost admits to his father in Chapter 18). As it is, he is her most perceptive critic and best friend.

NOTES AND GLOSSARY:

Bohemian: unconventional
Piccadilly: famous street in London
the Tower: the Tower of London
Turner: most original nineteenth-century English landscape painter (1775–1851)
Lord Nelson: English admiral killed at battle of Trafalgar (1805). A statue of Nelson stands on a column in Trafalgar Square, London
bric-à-brac: (*French*; in English usage) curiosities, assorted objects of some value
fête-champêtre: (*French*) picnic
Byron: English poet (1788–1824)
mountebank: a seller of quack medicines who attracts customers by joking and telling stories; a trickster or charlatan

Chapter 16

Caspar Goodwood arrives unexpectedly to see Isabel at Pratt's Hotel. Isabel is angry with Henrietta for telling him where to find her and with Goodwood for surprising her. Goodwood declares himself 'infernally in love' (p.155) with Isabel. She is touched by the intensity of his passion and by the romantic figure he presents as 'the strong man in pain' (p.156), but she can offer him no real hope. She gives him permission to visit her again after two years, but can promise him no reward except her gratitude for his absence until then. Goodwood agrees to go, but assures her that, at the end of two years, he will find her wherever she may be. Alone in her bedroom, Isabel kneels and hides her face in her arms.

COMMENTARY: Goodwood's love exerts an even greater pressure on Isabel than Warburton's. Forceful and insistent, he has an answer for all Isabel's objections. Isabel cannot be won, however. 'I wish to choose my fate,' she says (p.161).

Chapter 17

Isabel was neither praying nor weeping at the end of the previous chapter. She was vibrating with the sense of her own power in defending her freedom, first from Warburton, then from Goodwood.

When Henrietta returns from her dinner engagement, Isabel rebukes her for helping and encouraging Goodwood. Henrietta announces her intention of remaining in London to await an invitation from Mr Bantling's sister, Lady Pensil, to visit her home in Bedfordshire and 'see something of the inner life' (p.167).

Ralph arrives to say that Mr Touchett has become very ill. Isabel decides to return to Gardencourt with Ralph after he has seen the eminent doctor, Sir Matthew Hope. Henrietta tells Ralph about Isabel's visit from Goodwood whom, she says, she will advise not to give up.

COMMENTARY: Our attitude towards Isabel is subtly altered when we learn that she has enjoyed her exercise of power. Is she becoming 'hard' as she feared she might at the end of Chapter 12?

Not only is there a change in Isabel: the sudden illness of Mr Touchett augurs a change at Gardencourt too.

Chapter 18

Back at Gardencourt Isabel finds Madame Serena Merle, a friend of Mrs Touchett's from Florence. Ralph's ambiguous comments about Madame Merle's late husband imply that there is more to this lady than meets the eye.

Mr Touchett is dying. He is anxious about his son's future and wants Ralph to marry Isabel, which Ralph will not do. Ralph asks his father to alter the will so that half of the inheritance intended for him will be left to Isabel. Financial independence will free her of the need to marry for security. Mr Touchett has doubts—if Isabel is rich she may be married for her money—but he agrees.

COMMENTARY: When Mr Touchett asks Ralph if he is in love with Isabel, Ralph replies, 'No, I'm not in love with her; but I should be if—if certain things were different' (p.181). The 'things' Ralph has in mind are his own poor health and Isabel's love of freedom. As he cannot marry her himself, he does the next best thing in making it possible for her to achieve complete independence. Mr Touchett's money will 'put a little wind in her sails' (p.182). She will be able 'to meet the requirements of her imagination' (p.183) without counting the cost. The gain to Ralph will be the satisfaction of seeing Isabel as free as she wants to be, and the pleasure of observing what she does with her freedom.

NOTES AND GLOSSARY:
Schubert: Austrian composer (1797–1828)
du bout des doigts: (*French*) with the finger tips; softly
Brooklyn navy-yard: US navy dockyard in the borough of Brooklyn, New York City
Juno: principal Roman goddess
Niobe: in Greek mythology, a woman whom the gods turned to stone for boasting

Chapter 19

During Mr Touchett's illness, Isabel and Madame Merle are often together. Isabel comes to regard her new friend as a model of taste and wisdom, although Madame Merle suggests that her life has been a disappointment. Isabel suspects that there is something between Madame Merle and Ralph, but prefers not to know about it.

Madame Merle tells Isabel about her friend, Gilbert Osmond, who lives in Florence with his daughter. Mr Osmond is a man with 'no career, no name, no position, no fortune, no past, no future, no anything' (p.197). In other words, the clever Mr Osmond is occupied with being himself, free from all limitations, in a way likely to appeal to Isabel. Madame Merle promises to introduce Isabel to him.

Henrietta has not, after all, been invited to visit Lady Pensil. Mr Bantling is encouraging her to go to France, and it seems probable that he will accompany her.

A few days after Madame Merle's departure from Gardencourt, Mr Touchett dies.

COMMENTARY: Most of this chapter is concerned with Madame Merle and the dazzling impression she makes on Isabel. The reader is likely to have reservations about this new character. She is rather too knowing and sophisticated, too polished to be true. One of her opinions is especially important in relation to what follows in the novel. Every individual, she says, is made up of a 'cluster of appurtenances'. Madame Merle explains: 'One's self—for other people—is one's expression of one's self; and one's house, one's furniture, one's garments, the books one reads, the company one keeps—these things are all expressive' (p.201).

Isabel says that such things could never express her; but Madame Merle is not to be argued with on the subject.

NOTES AND GLOSSARY:

carte blanche: (*French*; in English usage) complete freedom
je viens de loin: (*French*) I have come a long way
je vous demande un peu: (*French*) I ask you!
carrière: (*French*) career
tout bêtement: (*French*) very stupidly
pied-à-terre: (*French*; in English usage) modest lodging; a place to stay
cluster of appurtenances: collection of things to which a person is attached

---

Chapter 20

Two weeks later Madame Merle arrives at the house in Winchester Square. The house is up for sale and Mrs Touchett is preparing to go to Paris with Isabel. On hearing that Mr Touchett has left Isabel a fortune of about seventy thousand pounds, Madame Merle mistakenly supposes that Isabel has been a 'clever creature' (p.208) in persuading her uncle to alter his will in her favour.

Exhausted by the strain of his father's death, Ralph is on his way to the warmer climate of the Riviera.

In Paris Isabel meets people who seem to lead lives of dull luxury. The most interesting of them is Edward (Ned) Rosier, whom she had met when they were both children. Henrietta has been energetically sight-seeing with Mr Bantling. She fears Isabel's new wealth may separate her from reality and confine her to a world of dreams.

COMMENTARY: Madame Merle is jealous of those who are to benefit from Mr Touchett's will. Another warning signal is her belief that Isabel must have manipulated her uncle into leaving her the money. We deduce that Madame Merle is all too familiar with such methods.

As the novel progresses, Henrietta is developing into a more likeable and substantial character. She still says silly things and she is inconsistent: she disapproves of idle Englishmen but makes an exception of Mr Bantling because she finds him agreeable and useful; but she shows insight when she warns Isabel that her money may encourage her to take 'romantic views' (p.217).

NOTES AND GLOSSARY:

a Cimabue Madonna: a picture of the Virgin Mary by the Italian painter Cimabue (*c*.1250–1302)

upon the skirts of the Champs Elysées: close to the Champs Elysées, a wide, tree-lined avenue in Paris, famous for its shops and cafés

Louis Philippe: King of France (1830–48)

Tuileries: French royal residence until 1871

bonne: (*French*) maid

Almanack de Gotha: a French annual giving genealogical, diplomatic, and statistical information about all states and countries

sans blague: (*French*) joking apart

je ne vous dis que ça!: (*French*) let's leave it at that!

salon: (*French*) drawing-room

the American procédure: (*French*) the American legal system

Chapter 21

Ralph has gone for the winter to San Remo in north-western Italy. Isabel and Mrs Touchett visit him on their way to Florence. Ralph admits to Isabel that he discussed her inheritance with his father, but does not reveal that it was his idea. He urges Isabel to enjoy her freedom. 'Spread your wings,' he advises her (p.222).

Isabel is somewhat afraid of the responsibilities that go with the freedom her money makes possible, but she looks forward to seeing Italy which seems to her 'a land of promise' (p.223). At times she thinks of Warburton and Goodwood, but 'these images of energy' (p.224) are fading into the background of her life. She realises, however, that one day she may be grateful for the security offered by Goodwood.

COMMENTARY: Now that Mr Touchett's money has given Isabel her freedom, she is nervous about using it properly. She is still the romantic in her idea of Italy but a new quality of self-doubt appears in her. One day she may come to the end of her quest for experience. If so, Caspar Goodwood's simple strength may appeal to her as a shelter from the world. In one of the key images of the novel Henry James describes the security Goodwood represents to Isabel's imagination as 'a clear and quiet harbour enclosed by a brave granite breakwater' to protect her from the open sea of life (p.225).

NOTES AND GLOSSARY:
dame de compagnie: (*French*) lady's companion

Chapter 22

Gilbert Osmond's house just outside Florence is a charming old villa overlooking the valley of the river Arno. It is furnished in the best taste by a cultured man who has 'studied style' (p.228). Osmond's fifteen-year-old daughter, Pansy, has been brought home from her convent school in Rome by two nuns.

Madame Merle arrives and although Osmond is surprised to see her, it soon becomes clear that these two know each other well. Madame Merle has visited Pansy at her convent and takes an intense interest in the girl, holding her back when Pansy would prefer to go out with her father to bid the nuns good-bye.

When Pansy is sent out to the garden, Madame Merle and Osmond talk like people who know each other in terms of a shared, bitter past. It seems as much a contest as a conversation. Madame Merle wants Osmond to meet—and marry—Isabel Archer. She tells Osmond that Isabel is the woman he needs. She will fill all his 'requirements' (p.240).

COMMENTARY: Henry James takes us from Isabel's image of the safe Caspar Goodwood at the end of the previous chapter, into an account of the cultivated but sinister Osmond.

This man is clearly dangerous. His intelligent eyes are 'hard' (p.228), and we remember that Isabel was worried at the end of Chapter 12 by the thought that she might be becoming 'hard' (p.111). Another warning about Osmond is given by his calling Ralph Touchett a 'jackanapes' (p.243). We know Ralph well enough to be suspicious of anyone who so misjudges him.

Osmond's house, although old, strikes us as a set piece manufactured by a man who wishes his taste to be admired. It is in contrast to Garden-court, which has evolved through four centuries of English history.

NOTES AND GLOSSARY:
Ce n'est pas ma partie: (*French*) It is not my doing
ces dames: (*French*) these ladies
ma mère: (*French*) my mother
gentille: (*French*) pleasingly pretty
La convent n'est pas comme le monde, monsieur: (*French*) The convent is not like the world, sir
Le monde y gagnera: (*French*) It will be the world's gain
mamman: (*French*) 'mother', familiar term implying affection
Que Dieu vous garde, ma fille: (*French*) May God protect you, my daughter

Je vous salve, mesdames: (*French*) My greetings to you, ladies
mignonne: (*French*) darling
En écus bien comptés?: (*French*) In ready money?
jackanapes: foolish, ape-like person

Chapter 23

Isabel is delighted by the artistic riches and historic buildings of Florence. Osmond calls on Madame Merle, who introduces him to Isabel. Isabel will not be drawn into conversation, but Osmond invites her to visit his home with Madame Merle.

Ralph tells Isabel that Osmond is a 'vague, unexplained American' who hates vulgarity (p.249). Osmond's wife is dead and his income is small. Ralph warns Isabel about Osmond's sister, but seems deliberately vague in what he says both about Osmond and about Madame Merle who, he suggests, is 'too complete', too accomplished, to be true.

COMMENTARY: We suspect that Ralph could say more about Osmond and Madame Merle if he chose, but he does not wish to interfere with Isabel's own perceptions of them. 'Judge everyone and everything for yourself,' he tells her. He is helping her to be free.

NOTES AND GLOSSARY:
cicerone: (*Italian*; in English usage) guide
de confiance: (*French*) with confidence
négociant: (*French*) merchant

Chapter 24

Isabel and Madame Merle visit Osmond at his villa. Pansy is there too, with Osmond's fashionable sister, the Countess Gemini, a foolish, gossipy woman. Osmond has devoted himself to the appreciation of 'art and beauty and history' (p.262). He is a connoisseur, a man who concentrates on his own perceptions. Ralph is a bit like this, in a humorous way. There are other aspects to Ralph, but Osmond's whole character seems involved in being this kind of man.

COMMENTARY: In Chapter 19 Isabel disagreed with Madame Merle's theory that everyone is made up of 'things', 'some cluster of appurtenances' (p.201). Yet here is Isabel liking a man who seems to express himself through pictures, medallions and tapestries. Even Pansy seems to be just another item in his collection. Isabel thinks she finds the man interesting, independently of his things, but we wonder if she herself will become another of Osmond's possessions.

Notice the care James takes in selecting what Countess Gemini calls Osmond's 'favourite subjects' (p.259). Osmond's interest in these figures suggests a man of deliberate refinement who is determined not to be thought ordinary, or vulgarly modern. (Compare Warburton's interest in the British politics of his own day, and Goodwood's involvement in the cotton industry. They are responsible men of the world; Osmond accepts no responsibility except that of pleasing himself.)

NOTES AND GLOSSARY:

bibelots:	(*French*) curios, knick-knacks
Machiavelli:	Italian political theorist with a reputation for cynicism (1469–1527)
Vittoria Colonna:	Italian poetess, especially renowned for her association with famous contemporaries including Michelangelo (1492–1547)
Metastasio:	Italian librettist (1698–1782)
Correggio:	leading painter of the Italian Renaissance whose work is often very sensuous in style (1494–1534)

Chapter 25

While Osmond talks to Isabel, Countess Gemini tells Madame Merle that she sees through her plan of bringing the two together, and warns Madame Merle that she intends to speak to Isabel about it. At first Madame Merle pretends not to understand what her companion means, but the Countess will not be put off. She says that Madame Merle and Osmond are 'capable of anything'. Individually they lack power, but together they are 'dangerous—like some chemical combination' (p.268). The Countess seems genuinely troubled by the thought that Isabel may be 'sacrificed' to Osmond (p.273).

COMMENTARY: Countess Gemini, like Henrietta Stackpole, is a superficial character who talks too much. Yet Henrietta accurately defined the hazards of Isabel's wealth, and the Countess sees exactly what is going on here.

NOTES AND GLOSSARY:

Longhi:	Italian portrait painter (1733–1813)
Goya:	Spanish painter (1746–1828)
toilette:	(*French*) dress

Chapter 26

Osmond becomes a frequent visitor to Mrs Touchett's house, the Palazzo Crescentini. Mrs Touchett thinks it would be ridiculous if Isabel refused an English lord and then married an American nobody. Ralph assures his mother that Isabel will not give up her freedom for Osmond: she is merely 'studying human nature' (p.275). Madame

Merle pretends to be surprised when Mrs Touchett asks her if Osmond is courting Isabel, and agrees to question him.

Isabel finds Osmond increasingly interesting and his daughter, Pansy, appealingly innocent, 'like a sheet of blank paper' (p.278). Mrs Touchett thinks Countess Gemini is like a sheet of paper too, but one much written on, with many blots. Madame Merle blames the Countess's silliness on her unhappy marriage.

Henrietta arrives in Florence, preceded by Mr Bantling, on her way to Rome. Ralph proposes that Isabel should go to Rome with her. Osmond prompts Isabel to invite him to visit her there. In a discussion about what to do with Pansy it becomes clear that he likes talking to Isabel about his domestic arrangements.

Osmond and Madame Merle meet at Countess Gemini's. Madame Merle does not like the idea of casting Isabel into an 'abyss' (p.286) through her plot to make her marry Osmond. Although Osmond thinks Isabel 'very charming' and 'graceful' he says her 'ideas' are 'bad'. This is just as well, he says, 'if they must be sacrificed' (p.286). The implication is that if Isabel marries Osmond, only his ideas will matter.

COMMENTARY: Ralph has too much faith in Isabel's ability to resist Osmond. Isabel's response to Pansy's innocence reminds us that Isabel herself is an innocent young American woman, no match for the sophisticated pair who are plotting against her. Osmond's comments to Madame Merle towards the end of the chapter make it clear that he thinks of Isabel cold-bloodedly as an object. As the Countess Gemini feared, Isabel's individuality will be 'sacrificed' if Osmond decides to add her to his collection.

NOTES AND GLOSSARY:

a fresh suitor at her gate: Ralph thinks of Isabel as a lady in a castle, defending her freedom from suitors who besiege her with offers of marriage

parley:	conference with an enemy
Val d'Arno:	Valley of the Arno
ingénue:	(*French*) artless girl
jeune fille:	(*French*) young girl
Tasso:	Italian author (1544–95)
Whyte-Melville:	English novelist (1821–78), educated at Eton
Dame:	(*French*) Madame

Chapter 27

Rome casts its spell on Isabel's imagination. On a visit to the Forum she is left alone for a short time and is suddenly confronted by Lord Warburton. His surprise at the meeting is equal to hers. Again he declares his love for her. Isabel likes and admires him but will not marry him, although she confesses that she is 'afraid' (p.292) of him. Warburton promises to say no more about his feelings and they agree to be friends.

The next day Isabel goes with her companions to St Peter's. Warburton is there and Osmond appears. Isabel has been impressed by the 'splendid immensity' (p.295) of the basilica but Osmond says he does not like it because it makes him feel small, 'like an atom' (p.296). When Isabel jokingly says he ought to be a Pope, Osmond replies, 'Ah, I should have enjoyed that' (p.297).

Ralph tells Warburton that Osmond is 'awfully clever', and suggests that the only way of keeping Isabel from marrying him is to do 'nothing to prevent it' (p.297).

COMMENTARY: St Peter's affords a telling contrast between Isabel and Osmond. The romantic Isabel finds the immensity of the basilica 'splendid': it gives her imagination 'space to soar' (p.295). Osmond feels dwarfed by the vastness of the place: he would rather be a Pope than an atom.

The coincidence of Lord Warburton's meeting with Isabel invites us to compare 'this fine specimen' (p.289) of an English lord, whose hand Isabel refuses, with the egotistical Osmond, whose hand she seems in danger of accepting. Even Ralph is worried now.

NOTES AND GLOSSARY:
Murray: a guide-book by John Murray (1808–92)
Forum: place of assembly in ancient Rome
Capitol: temple of Jupiter
Clapham Junction: railway junction near London

Chapter 28

Warburton visits Isabel and her friends at the opera. Osmond is curious about Warburton and expresses envy of a man so handsome and privileged. Isabel recalls his envy of the Pope. Two days later Warburton bids Isabel good-bye. He finds it impossible to see her and say nothing about his love for her. Rather than break his promise of silence, he is leaving Rome.

Isabel's rejection of Warburton makes her more attractive to Osmond.

COMMENTARY: Osmond now regards Isabel as eligible to 'figure in his collection of choice objects' (p.304). Declining the hand of Lord Warburton has made her a rarity, fit to be included among his possessions.

NOTES AND GLOSSARY:
Verdi: Italian composer of operas (1813–1901)
the lion of the collection: the most important exhibit

statue of the Dying Gladiator: symbolises the 'dying' of Warburton's hopes as a suitor competing for Isabel's love

Antinous and the Faun: Antinous, a favourite of the emperor Hadrian, sought to propitiate the gods with the sacrifice of a faun and, after his death, became the centre of a cult. Here the figure of Antinous symbolises Osmond's self-importance; the faun suggests Osmond's sacrifice of the innocent Isabel

---

Chapter 29

Even Ralph admits that Osmond can make himself good company. Osmond writes a sonnet entitled 'Rome Revisited' and shows it to Isabel. Isabel decides to go to Bellaggio with her aunt.

Osmond declares his love for Isabel. Tears come to her eyes and she has a sense within herself of 'inspired and trustful passion' (p.310). Osmond elicits her promise to visit Pansy at his house in Florence—he is to remain in Rome for a few more days. He leaves Isabel in a state of emotion which is 'very still, very deep' (p.312), but she is also rather unsure and apprehensive.

COMMENTARY: Notice the reference to Osmond's 'style' towards the end of the chapter's second paragraph. The implication is that Osmond values form more than content. A similar idea is contained in his remark to Isabel that 'one ought to make one's life a work of art' (pp.307–8). This suggests that a person's life should be not morally good or useful, but aesthetically pleasing. It should look good. Osmond tells Isabel, 'No, I'm not conventional: I'm convention itself' (p.312). This implies not merely that he conducts his life according to accepted rules of correct social behaviour, but that he is himself the perfect model of these rules. It is a mark of Isabel's innocence that she does not understand the full implications of what Osmond is saying.

Osmond is not at ease with Isabel's vitality and independence: he prefers to see her when she is 'tired and satiated', or when she is least herself. At the same time he seems to realise that he must give her time, and not press her freedom too hard.

The last paragraph of the chapter tells us that Isabel had anticipated his declaration, but that she now feels strangely hesitant. The way ahead looks rather dark, doubtful, even 'slightly treacherous' (p.313).

NOTES AND GLOSSARY:

Ampère: French historian, philologist and Romantic poet (1800–64)

Chapter 30

After some discussion with Madame Merle, Isabel visits Pansy, who tells her, 'Of everyone who comes here I like you the best' (p.316). Isabel is convinced that Pansy really is as innocent as she seems. Pansy speaks as though the purpose of her life is to please her father, but admits that she misses Madame Catherine, her teacher at the convent, 'almost more' than Osmond (p.316). Her days are completely regulated by instructions left by her father.

Isabel resists the temptation to talk too much about Osmond to Pansy, though she realises it would give her 'passionate pleasure' (p.318) to do so. When she leaves after an hour, Pansy says she will always expect Isabel's return.

COMMENTARY: Madame Merle suggests that it might not be proper for Isabel to go alone to see Pansy, because people do not know that Osmond is in Rome and might think Isabel was visiting him. By saying this Madame Merle is cleverly encouraging Isabel to think of the visit as a token of her growing commitment to Osmond.

The description of Pansy as 'a blank page, a pure white surface' suggests that the child lacks a mind of her own ('blank') and that she is innocent ('pure white') (p.315). While Osmond is away in Rome he controls Pansy—and keeps her 'blank'—by the instructions he leaves behind. He supplies the form of her life so completely that she is prevented from developing any content of her own.

NOTES AND GLOSSARY:
Ah, comme cela se trouve!: (*French*) Oh, how convenient!
dot: (*French*) dowry
portone: (*Italian*) outer door

Chapter 31

While Isabel awaits a visitor at her aunt's house in Florence, she surveys the events of the year that has passed since her visit to Pansy. She believes she has gained much more knowledge of life than she could have expected two years ago when she first arrived at Gardencourt as a 'frivolous young woman from Albany' (p.319).

She recalls the five-month visit of her sister, Lily Ludlow. Lily had thought Isabel might go back with her to America, but neither New York City nor Paris now has any appeal for Isabel. She had said good-bye to the Ludlows in London and then, with a heightened sense of freedom, returned to Rome.

With Madame Merle she had made a three-month tour of Greece, Turkey and Egypt. Her intimacy with Madame Merle developed on the trip, but she came to feel that her friend's ideas about right and wrong were different from her own, and possibly inferior. The thought that Madame Merle did not understand her made her uncomfortable.

At the end of March she returned to Rome and lodged with Madame Merle. Osmond came from Florence and saw her every day. At the end of April she went to be with her aunt in Florence. Ralph is expected to arrive soon from Corfu where he has spent the winter.

COMMENTARY: This chapter shows Isabel enjoying her freedom and exercising her power of choice. She chooses to travel; she chooses not to return to America, not to like Paris. Each act of choice makes her more confident, and she is self-assured enough to have doubts about Madame Merle. This prompts us to hope that she will discover Madame Merle's treachery and Gilbert Osmond's true nature before it is too late.

NOTES AND GLOSSARY:
éprouvée: (*French*) experienced

Chapter 32

Isabel's visitor is Caspar Goodwood. He has come from New York immediately on receiving a letter from Isabel in which she tells him of her engagement to Osmond. Isabel says she wishes he had not come. She is engaged to a man with neither money nor importance in whom Goodwood should not 'try to take an interest' (p.329).

Goodwood realises that this is an insulting way of saying that he is incapable of appreciating someone as fine as Osmond. Now that he has seen Isabel once more and heard her voice, Goodwood departs, promising to leave Florence the next day. After he has gone, Isabel bursts into tears.

COMMENTARY: The previous chapter left the reader hoping that Isabel would retreat from her involvement with Osmond. Now it is clearly too late.

Chapter 33

Mrs Touchett is bitterly disappointed in Isabel's engagement, and angry with Madame Merle for deceiving her. Isabel will not explain her reasons for choosing to marry Osmond.

Ralph arrives two days later. His health has deteriorated and the news of Isabel's engagement depresses him deeply.

Isabel hires a carriage of her own and drives every morning to meet Osmond in the Cascine, an area of open land just outside Florence.

COMMENTARY: This chapter is about loss. Ralph has suffered the 'complete loss of his health' (p.337) and Isabel has lost herself through her engagement to Osmond. Ralph realises now that he has misjudged Isabel's capacity for freedom: 'the person in the world in whom he was most interested was lost' (pp.338–9). Henry James brings Ralph's illness and Isabel's engagement together in the reader's mind, as if to suggest that Ralph's life depends on Isabel's freedom.

Chapter 34

Ralph tells Isabel he has been trying to express to himself what he thinks about her engagement. He regards her as 'caught' and about to be 'put in a cage' (p.341). (Compare Isabel's reaction to Warburton's proposal in Chapter 12, where she is likened to a creature 'caught' in a 'vast cage'; p.108.) Ralph is surprised by her willingness to surrender her liberty to a man who seems 'small . . . narrow, selfish' (p.345). Isabel says that Ralph has gone too far when he calls Osmond 'a sterile dilettante' (a man who amuses himself with cultural matters but produces nothing; p.345). Ralph answers that he has told Isabel his opinion because he loves her, but 'without hope' (p.346) either of winning her for himself or influencing her by what he says.

Isabel defends her choice of Osmond. She admires him precisely because he does not wish to be important. She sees him as 'a very lonely, a very cultivated and a very honest man' (p.347).

Isabel ends her conversation with Ralph by promising that she will not complain to him if her marriage to Osmond brings her trouble.

COMMENTARY: The reader should recognise the genuine nobility of Isabel's reply to Ralph. Here she is a truly romantic heroine for whom we are meant to feel sympathy and admiration. The tragic irony, of course, is that she is in love with her idea of Osmond.

NOTES AND GLOSSARY:

Terpsichore: one of the nine Greek Muses, patron of dancing and lyric poetry

Bernini: Italian sculptor (1562–1629)

Chapter 35

Isabel's engagement isolates her from her friends and relations but she reflects that one marries to please oneself, not to gain approval from others. Osmond realises that Mrs Touchett and Ralph suspect him of marrying Isabel for her money. He is grateful to Madame Merle and delighted about Isabel's money, as he is by everything about her.

Pansy is happy about the engagement, chiefly for her father's sake but also for her own. Countess Gemini is pleased by the prospect of having Isabel as a sister-in-law, but cannot pretend that she expects her to be happy. The Countess's own experience has taught her to regard marriage as 'a steel trap' (p.356).

COMMENTARY: Osmond behaves admirably to Isabel during their engagement, but he thinks about her in alarming terms. She is a valuable 'present' from Madame Merle (p.350). Her intelligence is to be 'a silver plate' (p.350) to mirror his own thought and make it richer, like music added to words. Isabel will both decorate his home and flatter his egotism. Pansy will 'amuse' them both (p.352).

Chapter 36

One afternoon in November 1876 Edward Rosier, Isabel's old acquaintance from Paris, comes to see Madame Merle. He asks her to help him win the hand of Pansy Osmond, whom he had met at St Moritz in the summer. Rosier gets on well with Madame Merle: they share a taste for artistic things and fine old lace. Madame Merle agrees to help him. She approves of his income of forty thousand francs and his 'nice' character, but advises him that Osmond may think differently and warns him not to approach Mrs Osmond on the subject.

COMMENTARY: The conversation between Rosier and Madame Merle gives us our first glimpse of Isabel's three-year-old marriage. Madame Merle confirms that Isabel is very fond of Pansy, but emphasises that Mr and Mrs Osmond generally disagree: 'They think quite differently.'

We have already commented on the significance of houses in the novel (see the Commentaries for Chapters 1, 3 and 22). Gardencourt was secure and kindly; Osmond's villa in Florence expressed his worship of taste. The Osmonds' house in Rome is a 'dark and massive structure', ominously called the Palazzo Roccanera ('Black Rock Palace'). Rosier thinks of it as a 'dungeon' in which Pansy is captive. We wonder if Isabel, too, leads the life of a prisoner.

NOTES AND GLOSSARY:
Dresden-china shepherdess: valuable porcelain figurine of a shepherdess made at the famous factory near Dresden
belle-mère: (*French*) step-mother
faience: (*French*) crockery
parti: (*French*) suitable match
Gardez-vous-en bien!: (*French*) Be very careful!
Caravaggio: Italian painter (1573–1610)
in the piano nobile: (*Italian*) on the main floor

Chapter 37

Rosier attends a social evening at the Palazzo Roccanera. Osmond greets him coldly and implicitly refers to Pansy when he says, 'No, I'm not thinking of parting with anything at all' (p.367). Rosier is further put off by Isabel. Pansy welcomes his expressions of affection and dutifully insists that her father be told about the young man's feelings.

Madame Merle arrives and speaks to Osmond about Rosier's interest in Pansy. Osmond finds Rosier boring and contemptible—'a donkey' (p.373). Madame Merle tells Osmond that Pansy likes Rosier, but Osmond does not care. Madame Merle realises that Rosier has declared himself to Pansy despite his promise that he would not do so. She is severe with him, but instructs him to come to her the following afternoon.

Rosier tells Isabel that Pansy and he have 'come to an understanding' (p.375). Isabel offers no hope: 'You're not rich enough' she says (p.375). When Rosier replies that Pansy does not care about money, Isabel answers that Osmond does. 'Ah yes, he has proved that!' exclaims Rosier (p.375). The implication that Osmond married her for her money offends Isabel. Rosier apologises for the insult. Isabel repeats that she has no power to help him.

COMMENTARY: Osmond's heartlessness is evident in his total disregard for Pansy's feelings. When, at the end of the chapter, Isabel tells Rosier that she cannot help him, Henry James observes, 'Her manner was almost passionate' (p.376). We deduce that Isabel's helplessness extends beyond the matter of Pansy's marriage. Ralph's prophecy seems to have come true: Isabel has been 'put into a cage' (p.341).

NOTES AND GLOSSARY:

Capo di Monte: a valuable soft porcelain produced in Naples and Madrid in the eighteenth century

an Infanta of Velazquez: a young girl painted by the Spanish artist Velazquez (1599-1660). James is probably thinking of the famous painting the *Infanta Margarita*

salottino: (*Italian*) small sitting-room

Chapter 38

Madame Merle tells Rosier to have patience: Osmond may change his mind. On the following Thursday, however, Osmond indicates to Rosier that he is not good enough for Pansy, who has now ceased to think of him. Rosier tells Isabel that her husband is 'awfully cold-blooded' (p.379).

Lord Warburton arrives unexpectedly. He has come to Rome with

Ralph whose health is rapidly worsening and who thinks he will be more comfortable in Sicily. Isabel is eager to see Ralph, but Warburton advises her to wait until the next morning. Warburton makes no embarrassing references to the past. He notices Pansy and thinks her charming.

Pansy tells Rosier that her father has forbidden her to marry him, even to speak to him. She says she will not give him up, but they must be patient. Pansy thinks Mrs Osmond will help them because 'She's not afraid of anyone' (p.387).

COMMENTARY: Lord Warburton's high position, social conscience and kindly character are in vivid contrast to Osmond's dependence on Isabel's money and his cold-blooded treatment of other people. Warburton is now a statesman in British politics; Osmond has a 'genius for upholstery' (p.385).

The further deterioration in Ralph Touchett's health develops the connection between Ralph and Isabel referred to in the Commentary for Chapter 33. As Isabel becomes more imprisoned in her marriage, Ralph grows more ill.

Chapter 39

In Chapter 34 Ralph told Isabel what a low opinion he had of Osmond. After that, as Osmond's wife, she could surely no longer be his friend. Ralph had attended the wedding in Rome and continued to predict a bleak future for Isabel. After nearly two years of marriage she had lost not only her child but also her mental vitality, her curiosity about life. She appears more physically active than ever, but her individuality seems masked. She now represents not herself but her husband.

Ralph realises that Isabel has married a charlatan. Osmond pretends not to care about worldly things and to live only for essential values, but this is just a pose to gain people's attention. The trick has worked on Isabel who, sadly, embodies the 'gullible world' (p.394).

Ralph decides to stay in Rome and see more of Isabel. Warburton, too, will stay in Rome. He has begun to think that he might marry Pansy, in spite of the difference in their ages. Ralph angers Warburton by suggesting that his friend is thinking of marrying Pansy as a way of being close to Isabel.

COMMENTARY: Ralph's judgement of Osmond demonstrates again that he is the most perceptive character in the novel. Henry James now comments explicitly on the connection between Isabel's career and Ralph's hold on life: 'What kept Ralph alive was simply the fact that he had not yet seen enough of the person in whom he was most interested: he was not yet satisfied' (p.395).

NOTES AND GLOSSARY:

in petto: (*Italian*) in his heart of hearts; privately to himself

Campagna: plain surrounding the city of Rome

between Scylla and Charybdis: the conflict between the devouring monster (Scylla) and the whirlpool (Charybdis); the phrase is used to describe an insoluble problem

Proserpine: carried off to the underworld by Pluto (Hades) while she was gathering flowers in the vale of Enna in Sicily

An, vous m'en demandez trop!: (*French*) You're asking too much of me!

Chapter 40

Madame Merle has been frequently absent from Rome since Isabel's marriage. Isabel often feels depressed and wishes her friend were available to teach her the art of living 'by reason and by wisdom' (p.401). Isabel does not share Mrs Touchett's conviction that Madame Merle arranged her marriage, but she is now unable to explain to herself how it happened.

Returning one day from a walk with Pansy, Isabel surprises Osmond and Madame Merle sharing 'a sort of familiar silence' (p.408), which suggested a high degree of intimacy. When Osmond leaves, Madame Merle says she wants no more to do with the 'love-affairs of Miss Pansy and Mr Edward Rosier' (p.410). She then encourages Isabel to influence Lord Warburton to marry Pansy.

COMMENTARY: Although Isabel refuses to believe that Madame Merle is responsible for her marriage, she can no longer believe that it was purely a matter of her own choice. Her thinking of it as the work 'of nature, providence, fortune, of the eternal mystery of things' (p.403) means that she cannot sustain the idea of herself as truly free, even in the past.

NOTES AND GLOSSARY:

Pincian: *via Pinciana*, a fashionable street in Rome

Je n'y peux rien, moi!: (*French*) There's nothing I can do about it!

Chapter 41

That evening Lord Warburton pays one of his brief visits to the Osmond house and talks mainly to Pansy. Isabel now thinks he would be an excellent husband for her step-daughter, although she is still anxious about Rosier who has stopped visiting the Palazzo Roccanera.

Osmond tells Isabel that he wishes Warburton to marry Pansy. At first he professes confidence in the match: 'My daughter has only to sit perfectly quiet to become Lady Warburton' (p.420); but he goes on to tell Isabel that he expects her to use her influence with Warburton to bring him to the point of proposing.

COMMENTARY: Isabel's feelings after her marriage are brilliantly illustrated by one sentence in this chapter: 'She sometimes felt a sort of passion of tenderness for memories which had no other merit than that they belonged to her unmarried life' (p.419). Yet she still has a strong sense of duty to Osmond, tries to please him, and is anxious to 'play the part of a good wife' (p.415).

The conversation between Isabel and Osmond displays Osmond's arrogance, his ambition and his domination of Pansy. His taunting reference to Warburton's wooing of Isabel is the kind of cruelty we have come to expect from him.

NOTES AND GLOSSARY:
grist-tax: tax on corn
pellagra: (*Italian*) a chronic deficiency disease, common among the very poor

---

Chapter 42

Isabel sits up alone until four o'clock in the morning, thinking about her marriage. Osmond has given her a 'repulsive' task in requiring her to use her influence with Warburton (p.423). She echoes Ralph's misgiving at the end of Chapter 39 when she wonders if Warburton wants to marry Pansy simply to be closer to herself. The situation seems hopelessly confused, but she resolves not to worry about Warburton for the present.

Her life with Osmond is 'horrible' (p.433). They look at each other across a 'gulf': Osmond is not violent or, in any simple sense, cruel, but he seems to make everything he touches 'wither' (p.424). Isabel had married him because she thought him splendid—poor and lonely, yet noble. She had happily brought him the fortune left her by Mr Touchett because she thought he would put it to excellent use. This would make her feel less guilty about being rich. She still believes in the brilliance and cultivation of Osmond's mind, but realises that he has nothing but contempt for hers: 'he would have liked her to have nothing of her own but her pretty appearance' (p.428). The 'tradition' Osmond regards so highly means little more than a society in which lies and sexual infidelities are disguised by careful manners.

Isabel blames herself for being too reticent during her engagement, when she was under the spell of Osmond's charm. Now she sees that, under his charm, 'his egotism lay hidden like a serpent in a bank of flowers' (p.430). She supposes he hates her.

There is consolation in her renewed contact with Ralph, although she does not speak to him of her marriage. Ralph realises that she does not wish to give him the pain of knowing about her unhappiness.

When she gets up to go to bed, Isabel suddenly recalls the image of Osmond and Madame Merle as she had caught them unawares the previous afternoon, absorbed in each other.

COMMENTARY: Until this crucial chapter the reader has known much more than Isabel about Osmond's character and Madame Merle's duplicity. Isabel's unhappiness is appalling, yet it comes as a relief to find that she is, at last, aware of her situation. From now on, the chief interest of the novel will not be so much in what Isabel finds out as in how she copes with her predicament.

NOTES AND GLOSSARY:

A Unitarian preacher: a minister of the Unitarian Church who emphasises freedom and tolerance

Chapter 43

Isabel takes Pansy to a party where Rosier and Warburton are among the guests. Rosier is made even more miserable by the feeling that Isabel pities him but will not help him with Pansy.

Warburton invites Isabel to dance but she declines. While Pansy dances with various admirers, Warburton repeats his wish to marry 'the little maid', although he has not sent the letter he has written to her father. He shows a more credible interest in Isabel herself and is quick to sympathise with Rosier. For a brief moment, Isabel and Warburton look at each other in an 'extremely personal gaze', which seems to support Isabel's idea that Warburton wishes to be as near her as possible.

As she leaves the party with Pansy, Isabel tells Rosier she will do what little she can to help him. She also reminds Warburton to send his letter to Osmond.

COMMENTARY: In spite of her unhappy life with Osmond, Isabel dutifully stands guard over Pansy and is careful to be circumspect in her dealings with Warburton. It is clear that he is more interested in her than in her step-daughter, and this prompts us to wonder if Isabel might look to him for an escape from her unhappy marriage.

Chapter 44

Bored by life in Florence with her dreary husband, the Countess Gemini looks forward to visiting the Osmonds in Rome. She hopes that Isabel will have taken the dominant position in the marriage: it would please her to see Osmond 'over-topped' (p.450).

The Countess is flattered to receive a visit from Henrietta Stackpole who is disturbed by her suggestion that there may be something between Isabel and Lord Warburton. Henrietta decides to go at once to Rome but first calls on Caspar Goodwood, who is back in Florence. Goodwood agrees to go with her to Rome.

COMMENTARY: Just as Isabel accepts that her marriage is the precise kind she sought to avoid, she is made aware of Warburton's continued interest in her. Another reminder of what might have been is now about to approach her in the person of Caspar Goodwood.

NOTES AND GLOSSARY:

Creole: here, implying mixed ancestry originating in the French speakers of Louisiana

pension: (*French*) residential hotel; boarding-house

extremely grand seigneur: (*French*) very much the lord

c'est bien gentil!: (*French*) how very kind!

Ponte Vecchio: bridge crossing the River Arno, Florence

Chapter 45

Isabel knows that Osmond dislikes her seeing Ralph because he encourages her freedom of mind. She continues to visit Ralph, although she dreads an open break with Osmond which would proclaim their marriage a failure. She now asks Ralph about Warburton's interest in Pansy. Ralph is in no doubt that Warburton really cares for Isabel herself, but points out that Osmond may accuse her of jealousy if she does not encourage Warburton to marry Pansy.

Pansy tells Isabel that she wishes to marry Rosier. She will stay single rather than marry anyone else, but will not marry Rosier without Osmond's permission. Determined to carry out Osmond's instructions —but conscious of her own insincerity—Isabel advises Pansy to respect Osmond's wishes and to favour Warburton. Pansy is not to be talked out of her love for Rosier: he may not be a nobleman, like Lord Warburton, but he 'looks like one' (p.473).

COMMENTARY: Isabel still believes it her duty to be loyal to Osmond. Her marriage is still 'the single sacred act' of her life (p.463).

Chapter 46

Osmond accuses Isabel of being untrustworthy and complains that she has only pretended to encourage Warburton's interest in marrying Pansy.

Warburton arrives. He is on the point of returning to England but Ralph will not leave Rome until warmer weather comes. Warburton invites the Osmonds to visit him at Lockleigh in the autumn. He wishes to say good-bye to Pansy. When Osmond leaves the room Warburton urges Isabel to visit England.

Warburton bids Pansy good-bye and tells her how much he wishes her to be happy. He refers to Isabel as Pansy's 'guardian angel' (p.480).

Later that evening Osmond charges Isabel with deliberately humiliating him: she has put him in the position of a man who has tried to marry his daughter to a lord and failed. Isabel replies that she has acted as Osmond wishes, but that Pansy does not care for Warburton. Osmond again dismisses Pansy's feelings as of no importance. Amazed by her husband's attitude, Isabel is filled with pity for Pansy.

COMMENTARY: This chapter dramatises the increasing pace with which Isabel's marriage is disintegrating. Husband and wife now face each other as enemies.

Chapter 47

Henrietta tells Isabel that Goodwood is in Rome. Isabel feels guilty about her harsh treatment of him at their last meeting (Chapter 32). She hopes to have an opportunity to 'set herself right' (p.486) with him, but realises that she must conceal her unhappiness as it would distress him more than anyone. Henrietta tells Isabel that Goodwood suspects her of being unhappy, and talks about Mr Bantling's visit to America where he was especially fascinated by hotels and river steamers.

The private gulf between Osmond and Isabel is widened by Osmond's dislike of her friends: Ralph is a 'conceited ass', unfairly privileged because of his illness; Warburton has insolently inspected and discarded Pansy; Henrietta is 'a kind of monster' who 'talks as a steel pen writes' (pp.490–1).

Goodwood becomes a regular visitor to the Palazzo Roccanera where Osmond deliberately surprises Isabel by appearing to like him. At Isabel's request Goodwood goes to see Ralph who is now visited daily by Henrietta. Edward Rosier turns up again. Madame Merle returns from Naples and asks what Isabel has done with Lord Warburton.

COMMENTARY: Despite her admission to Henrietta that she is unhappy and ashamed of being so, Isabel regards herself as bound to Osmond. She could not bear the greater shame of announcing to the world that she had chosen wrongly. In this, Isabel remains true to her belief in the responsibilities of freedom: 'One must accept one's deeds' (p.488).

Chapter 48

Late in February Ralph feels ready to make the journey to Gardencourt
and accepts Henrietta's decision to go with him. Goodwood is to
accompany them at Isabel's request, although he realises that this is her
way of getting him to leave Rome.

Henrietta tells Countess Gemini that her suspicions about Isabel's
relations with Warburton are unfounded. The Countess supposes that
Pansy rejected Warburton because she thought Isabel cared for him.
Henrietta again tries to persuade Isabel to leave Osmond before he
spoils her character, but Isabel replies that she is taking care of herself
and points out that Henrietta can only speak so easily of a woman's
leaving her husband because she has never been married herself.

Isabel says good-bye to Ralph and tells him that he has been her 'best
friend' (p.504). Ralph says that she had given him a reason for living,
but that he is of no use to her now.

Goodwood remains suspicious about Isabel's marriage in spite of
Osmond's attempts to paint a picture of mutual adoration. Goodwood
again declares his love for Isabel and asks if he may spend his life pitying
her. Isabel replies: 'Don't give your life to it; but give a thought to it
every now and then' (p.513).

COMMENTARY: Osmond's hypocrisy is nowhere more evident than in
this chapter. He tries to make Goodwood believe that Isabel's marriage
is ideally happy, asserting his superiority by implying that Goodwood
could not have done as much for her. Osmond under-rates Goodwood's
intelligence, as he does Ralph's and Henrietta's.

Chapter 49

This chapter describes events prior to the Thursday evening of the
previous chapter.

On Madame Merle's return from Naples she asked Isabel why Lord
Warburton left Rome without proposing to Pansy. It dawned on Isabel
that Madame Merle's 'interest was identical with Osmond's' (p.515).
When Madame Merle admitted that she had 'everything' to do with
her, Isabel deduced that Mrs Touchett had been right: Madame Merle
had arranged her marriage to Osmond.

On the afternoon of Madame Merle's visit Isabel took a drive among
the ruins of Rome, where 'the ruin of her happiness seemed a less un-
natural catastrophe' (p.517). She faced the fact that Madame Merle
had been 'deeply false' (p.519) and that Osmond had married her for
her money. She wondered if he might now be satisfied with the money
and let her go.

On the same afternoon Osmond visited Madame Merle who felt remorse for her cruel treatment of Isabel that morning. She bitterly accused Osmond of making her as 'bad' as himself (p.523) and attacked his behaviour towards Isabel. Osmond remained cool and aloof, his attention seemingly more engaged by a small cup of Madame Merle's than by anything in her conversation. He said he only wanted Isabel to 'adore' him, and Madame Merle should not have put him into such a 'box' (p.524) by arranging his marriage.

COMMENTARY: As the corrupt world of experience closes around her, Isabel is hardly recognisable as the person who came to Europe from Albany, eager for 'a large acquaintance with human life' (p.519).

Osmond's capacity for self-deception is as great as his capacity for deceiving others. Clearly he would not have married Isabel without her money, but his vanity leads him to profess only a romantic disappointment. Osmond has a sharp eye for a tiny crack in Madame Merle's small porcelain cup. The implication is that for him the imperfection makes the cup worthless. In people, too, he demands absolute perfection according to his own standards.

NOTES AND GLOSSARY:
Eh moi donc?:   (*French*) What about me?

Chapter 50

Isabel sometimes takes the Countess Gemini on a tour of the Roman ruins to distract her sister-in-law's mind from gossip. One afternoon the Countess climbs to the top of the Coliseum with Pansy, while Isabel remains seated in the arena. Isabel is approached by Rosier who tells her that he has sold nearly all his *bibelots* (precious artistic objects) in order to be rich enough to please Osmond as a suitor for Pansy. Isabel cannot assure him that fifty thousand dollars will be enough, but tells him that he deserves to succeed. When the Countess and Pansy return, Isabel swiftly takes Pansy to their carriage. Pansy offers no resistance, but the 'spark of timid passion' (p.529) which Isabel sees in her eyes is a sign of her feelings towards Rosier.

About a week after this incident, Pansy tells Isabel that Osmond is sending her back to the convent. Osmond says he thinks Pansy needs a quiet period to think about the world in the right way. Isabel realises that Osmond is demonstrating his control of Pansy.

The Countess Gemini accuses Osmond of sending Pansy away to be beyond her influence. Rosier's devotion to Pansy has made the Countess believe in true love. Osmond says that if he had been worried about his sister's influence it would have been easier to send her away.

COMMENTARY: Compare Rosier and Osmond. When we first meet Rosier in Chapter 20 he is a self-centred young man who collects artistic things which will proclaim his good taste. Osmond's character as a connoisseur remains static, but Rosier's love for Pansy transforms him from a collector of things into a lover romantic enough to sell nearly all his possessions for the sake of his beloved. Pansy, however, is still her father's prime possession and her 'spark of passion' is only 'timid'.

NOTES AND GLOSSARY:

Baths of Titus: remains of Roman baths built in reign of the emperor Titus (AD 81)

Coliseum: or 'Colosseum'; ruins of giant amphitheatre, completed in AD 82; seated 50,000 spectators at gladiatorial and other contests

the Arnide: the women of Florence

En voilà, ma chère, une pose!: (*French*) What affectation, my dear!

simpaticissimo: (*Italian*) most attractive

Chapter 51

Isabel receives a telegram from Mrs Touchett: Ralph is dying at Gardencourt and wishes to see her. Osmond accuses her of liking Ralph simply because Ralph hates him, and he tells her that it would be 'dishonourable', 'indelicate' and 'indecent' (p.536) of her to make the journey to Gardencourt in opposition to his wishes. Their marriage may be disagreeable, but they both chose it. The only honourable thing, he says, is to 'accept the consequences of our actions' (p.537).

On her way to her own room Isabel meets Countess Gemini. Isabel tells her that Ralph is dying and that Osmond forbids her to go to him. The Countess expresses her sympathy. Alone in her room, Isabel reflects that, whatever differences there may be between Osmond and herself, he is right in his view of the obedience required by the 'tremendous vows' (p.540) of marriage.

The Countess resents Osmond's bullying Isabel who has always been kind to her. She comes to Isabel's room and tells her that Madame Merle is Pansy's mother: Osmond and Madame Merle had arranged addresses and dates so that the girl could be claimed as the daughter of Osmond's first wife. Madame Merle would not marry Osmond because she had greater ambitions; Osmond would not marry her because she had no money. Isabel was selected as a suitable wife for Osmond because she had money, and Madame Merle believed she would be good to Pansy.

After the Countess's revelations Isabel cries, 'Ah, I must see Ralph!'.

COMMENTARY: Isabel still accepts Osmond's view of marriage as a contract which is sacred and binding, a 'magnificent form' (p.537) even when the content is lacking. The ability to accept the truth of something spoken by a villain is a mark of moral discrimination and strength. The irony here is that in this situation it becomes a 'weakness' which at first prevents Isabel from defying Osmond and going immediately to Ralph. Osmond's 'art of eliciting any weakness' (p.538) recalls his finding the tiny crack in Madame Merle's coffee cup at the end of Chapter 49.

Isabel's decision to go to Ralph is not revenge for the way in which she has been victimised by Osmond and Madame Merle. Plunged into sadness by the news of Ralph's dying and by the Countess's story, she needs to see for the last time the one person who has both understood and loved her.

NOTES AND GLOSSARY:

Ça me dépasse: (*French*) It's beyond me
poverina: (*Italian*) poor little thing
at so awkward a pinch: in such a difficult emergency
cara mia: (*Italian*) my dear

Chapter 52

Before she leaves for England, Isabel goes to Pansy's convent to say good-bye. She is depressed by the prison-like atmosphere and startled to find Madame Merle there. Madame Merle suddenly realises that Isabel's attitude towards her has changed: she guesses that Isabel now knows her secret. Isabel has a sense of revenge as she imagines her old friend's dread of exposure, but decides to say nothing that might give Madame Merle an opportunity to defend herself.

Isabel realises sadly that Osmond's power over Pansy has been strengthened by association with the religious authority of the convent; the girl's slight resistance to her father's wishes is quite overcome. She will now give up Rosier and marry to please Osmond. Pansy seems frightened by the possibility that Isabel may not return from England and she abruptly announces that she does not like Madame Merle. Isabel promises her to come back.

Madame Merle has waited for Isabel to finish her visit to Pansy. She tells Isabel that Mr Touchett's legacy was Ralph's idea and that Isabel has Ralph to thank for making her 'a brilliant match' (p.559). (She means that if Ralph had not made her rich, Osmond would not have married her.)

Isabel says she would like not to see Madame Merle again. Madame Merle remarks that she will go to America.

COMMENTARY: When Pansy says she does not like Madame Merle she unknowingly rejects her mother. If Isabel abandons Pansy she will leave her without even a step-mother. Isabel's promise to come back signifies her acceptance of the role of Pansy's mother at a deeper level than before. She will always technically be Pansy's step-mother, but her feeling for the lonely girl makes her the only 'real' mother Pansy has.

Madame Merle's last blow is her most deadly. Ralph believed that money would make Isabel free, yet it was Mr Touchett's legacy which attracted Osmond. Has the condition of her freedom been the cause of her undoing? Has she ever been free?

NOTES AND GLOSSARY:
Elle éclaire la maison: (*French*) She lights up the house
Eh bien, chère Madame, qu'en pensez-vous?: (*French*) What are you thinking about, dear lady?

Chapter 53

Isabel arrives in London to be met by Henrietta and Mr Bantling. Hardly aware of the countries she passes through on her journey, she looks not outward at the springtime scenery, but inward at the wintry landscape of her life. She had set out from Gardencourt with vigour; now she returns for a rest. She envies Ralph the release from trouble that dying will bring, but senses that her own future will be long. To be human, it seems, is to suffer.

The news from Henrietta and Mr Bantling is that Ralph is resting quietly. Isabel agrees to spend the night with Henrietta in London and go to Gardencourt the next morning. She does not deny that her parting talk with Osmond was 'hellish' (p.565), as Henrietta supposes, and cannot explain why she promised Pansy she would return. She realises that Osmond's hatred of her coming to England will be 'a scene of the rest of my life' (p.565).

Henrietta is to marry Mr Bantling and settle in London. Isabel is surprised by the patriotic Henrietta's willingness to give up America, and momentarily disappointed that her friend is, after all, human, feminine and 'subject to common passions' (p.567). She realises, however, that if Henrietta is less exceptional than she had thought, Mr Bantling is original.

COMMENTARY: This chapter emphasises the contrast between Isabel's hard-earned view of life as 'full of the destruction of precious things' (p.562) and Henrietta's happy engagement to the genial Mr Bantling. James gives us a moment of relief from the tensions of Isabel's situation. He also reminds us that life holds other possibilities than those realised by Isabel. She is a 'special case'.

NOTES AND GLOSSARY:
Charing Cross: a main-line railway station in London

| **Etruscan figures:** | in Etruscan cremation, ashes of the dead were some-times placed in urns shaped like human figures |

Chapter 54

At Gardencourt Isabel is a stranger to the new servants and Mrs Touchett is not in evidence to welcome her. While she waits for her aunt to appear Isabel thinks of the change in herself since she first came to the house some six years ago.

Mrs Touchett comes from sitting with Ralph. Over the mid-day meal she tells Isabel that Lord Warburton is soon to be married, and Isabel wonders how Osmond will take this news. Mrs Touchett asks Isabel about Madame Merle. Without giving details Isabel says that Madame Merle 'made a convenience' of her (p.573).

Isabel sits at Ralph's bedside, but for three days he is too weak for conversation. When he does speak he expresses his love for Isabel and his anxiety about her future. Ralph believes he has ruined her by arranging for her to be wealthy. Isabel agrees that Osmond had been in love with her but that he would not have married her if she had been poor.

The fact that Ralph and Isabel are now 'looking at the truth together' lifts them above the pain of this final meeting. Ralph tells Isabel to remember that she has been not merely loved but 'adored', and Isabel responds by giving him the name of 'brother' (p.578).

COMMENTARY: Even now Isabel is too proud to give her aunt a detailed account of how Madame Merle has exploited and humiliated her. Only with Ralph is she utterly without reserve. Ralph no longer hides behind his wit but frankly declares his adoration. In Chapter 48 Isabel called Ralph 'my best friend' (p.504); now her cry of 'Oh my brother' (p.578) acknowledges him as her true kin. It is their mutual recognition of the profound relationship between them that turns this death-bed scene into a victory.

Chapter 55

In Chapter 5 Ralph told Isabel that she might one day see the ghost of Gardencourt if she suffered enough. Just before dawn, after her last talk with him, Isabel sees a ghostly vision of Ralph hovering by her bed. She goes to his room and finds that he has died.

After the funeral she stays on at Gardencourt with her aunt, postponing her return to Rome, which she thinks of 'with a kind of spiritual shudder' (p.581). She cannot decide what to do. Warburton visits Mrs Touchett and is somewhat embarrassed to see Isabel. He renews his invitation to her to pay a visit to Lockleigh, but does not mention his engagement.

In the grounds of Gardencourt Isabel recognises the wooden bench where she had been sitting years ago, reading a letter from Goodwood, when Warburton came to propose marriage to her. Suddenly Goodwood stands before her and speaks to her with new force. Ralph has told him of Isabel's misery with Osmond and has asked him to do everything possible for her. Goodwood begs Isabel to turn from her husband —'the deadliest of fiends' (p.588)—and to put her trust in him.

Isabel is tempted to escape from her troubles, and to accept the refuge Goodwood offers. Weeping, she begs him to leave. He embraces her with a kiss 'like white lightning' (p.591) and she almost succumbs to his passion. After the kiss she is 'free', herself again, and, as she runs from Goodwood, she knows what she will do.

Goodwood looks for her in London two days later, but learns from Henrietta that she has left for Rome.

COMMENTARY: In Chapter 21 Isabel reflected that she might 'come to the end of the things that were not Caspar' (p.225). She has approached that point when, in this chapter, Caspar suddenly appears before her, urging her to accept the security of his love instead of going back to Osmond.

She resists Goodwood for two reasons. First, he appeals to her to regard herself as free, but life has taught Isabel to distrust superficial ideas of freedom; secondly, James describes Isabel's feelings for Goodwood in terms of dying, sinking, drowning (pp.590–1). The implication is that Goodwood almost renders Isabel unconscious.

In Henry James's world to live at all is to be conscious and, for Isabel, consciousness involves acknowledging her promise to Pansy and her marriage vows to Osmond. She must, therefore, go back to Rome.

NOTES AND GLOSSARY:

Whitsuntide: the week beginning with the seventh Sunday after Easter

Christie's: famous London auction rooms

Part 3

Commentary

HENRY JAMES'S PURPOSE is to paint Isabel Archer's portrait by placing 'the centre of the subject in the young woman's own consciousness' (p.xiii). The 'subject' of the novel is Isabel's progress from innocence to experience as she tries to live freely, fails, and achieves a deeper understanding of the meaning of freedom.

James enables us to share Isabel's point of view by revealing her thoughts and feelings to us, often commenting on them to guide our judgement. As a result we know more about her than she knows about herself. We also know more about the characters who affect her. This is James's method of maintaining a sense of Isabel's innocence, of preserving our sympathy for her as the victim of a conspiracy, and of keeping up the suspense.

This method of focusing on the consciousness of a single 'lighted figure' gives intensity to James's work. It is much easier to sympathise with one person than with several people in different situations. Richly populated novels such as Tolstoy's *War and Peace* or George Eliot's *Middlemarch* have their own special power, but they do not provide the kind of intensity found in James. They ask us to respond to so many characters, that our feelings for any individual character can never reach maximum intensity. There are too many claims on our interest and emotions.

In an essay on the life of George Eliot, James defines 'the basis of the story-teller's art' as 'the passion for the special case'. In *The Portrait of a Lady*, clearly, the 'special case' is Isabel Archer. It is her mind James shows us most intimately. (Chapter 42, which James thought 'the best thing in the book' (p.xvii), is made up entirely of Isabel's thoughts.) When other characters meet, it is Isabel they discuss, so that she is 'lit' even when she is not present. When we learn that Ralph Touchett has arranged for her to be rich and free, we look forward, as he does, to finding out what she will do with her freedom. When we see her refuse the marriage proposals of two good men, we worry with her, and when we discover that she is drawn to the villainous Gilbert Osmond, we hope that her perceptions of him will become keen enough to stop her before it is too late. Her mind, her story, her 'Portrait' hold our attention to the end.

Structure

The structure of the novel is the shape given to the plot. There are two kinds of structure in *The Portrait of a Lady*.

The *formal* structure arises from James's method of 'lighting' one central figure by showing her in relation to other characters. This gives the novel a circular shape. Isabel stands at the centre, ringed by the Touchetts, Caspar Goodwood, Lord Warburton, Henrietta Stackpole, Madame Merle, Gilbert Osmond and the rest. As each of these characters interacts with Isabel, her portrait becomes clearer until, at the end of the book, it is completely defined.

The *chronological* structure of the novel is basically linear, despite James's restrained use of flashback in chapters 3–6, 11, 13, 31, 36, 49. This divides the book into six sections.

Section 1: Chapters 1–6 (Introduction)

Chapter 1 prepares us for Isabel's entry in Chapter 2. Chapters 3–6 provide information about her American background, her qualities of mind, her rejection of Caspar Goodwood, and her expectations of Europe.

This section shows Isabel enjoying Gardencourt where she is liked by everyone, but James also reveals her faults and advises us to be 'tender' and 'expectant' (p.52).

Section 2: Chapters 7–21 (Exposition)

This section develops Isabel's relationship with Lord Warburton to the point of his proposal (Chapter 12) and her rejection of it (Chapter 13).

Henrietta Stackpole arrives (Chapter 10). She urges Isabel to remain true to her American origins and to look favourably on Caspar Goodwood who visits Isabel in London (Chapter 16), only to be rejected again.

Isabel meets and admires Madame Merle who promises to introduce her to Gilbert Osmond. Ralph persuades his father to leave Isabel a handsome legacy (Chapter 18). Mr Touchett dies. Isabel finds herself rich (Chapter 21) and prepares to go to Florence with her aunt.

Section 3: Chapters 22–32 (Development)

The scene shifts to Gilbert Osmond's house near Florence (Chapter 22). It is clear that a long-standing relationship exists between him and Madame Merle. Isabel is introduced to Osmond by Madame Merle. She visits him at his house and meets Pansy (Chapter 24).

The Countess Gemini realises that Madame Merle and Osmond are trying to manipulate Isabel into marriage (Chapter 25). Lord Warburton appears in Rome and speaks again of his love for Isabel (Chapter 27). Osmond declares himself in love with Isabel (Chapter 29).

Isabel travels for a year, returns to Italy and becomes engaged to Osmond. She writes to Goodwood of her engagement. Goodwood rushes to Florence. Isabel rejects him once more (Chapter 32).

Section 4: Chapters 33–42 (Consequences—I)

Isabel's engagement angers Mrs Touchett and makes Ralph more ill. Ralph tells Isabel what he thinks of Osmond (Chapters 33–4).

Madame Merle undertakes to assist Edward Rosier in his courtship of Pansy, but Isabel says she has no power to help him (Chapter 37).

Ralph Touchett and Lord Warburton arrive in Rome (Chapter 38) and decide to stay. Warburton considers marrying Pansy, but is really still attracted to Isabel.

Isabel recognises an intimacy between Osmond and Madame Merle (Chapter 40). Osmond instructs Isabel to encourage Warburton's interest in Pansy. Isabel faces the fact that her life with Osmond is 'horrible' (Chapter 42).

Section 5: Chapters 43–52 (Consequences—II)

This section is distinguished from the previous one by the fact that Isabel now sees the reality of her situation.

Isabel tries to encourage Warburton's interest in Pansy, but Pansy is loyal to her feelings for Rosier. Warburton leaves Rome and Osmond blames Isabel for failing (Chapters 43–6).

Goodwood and Henrietta come to Rome and accompany Ralph home to Gardencourt (Chapter 48).

Ralph, now dying, sends for Isabel. Osmond opposes Isabel's going. Countess Gemini tells Isabel how Osmond and Madame Merle conspired to make her marry Osmond and reveals that Madame Merle is Pansy's mother (Chapter 51).

Isabel decides to go to Ralph. First, she says good-bye to Pansy and promises to return.

Section 6: Chapters 53–55 (Conclusions)

Isabel is met in London by Henrietta and Mr Bantling who are now engaged (Chapter 53). At Gardencourt she and Ralph face the truth together (Chapter 54). Ralph dies. Isabel rejects Goodwood's attempt to persuade her to go away with him. She returns to Rome (Chapter 55).

Language

Henry James's vocabulary is not unusual; it is his use of words, the ways in which he combines them, that makes his style distinctive.

He often says things indirectly in order to express more meaning than a simple statement of fact could convey. On the first page of *The Portrait of a Lady* James refers to afternoon tea as a 'little feast' and to cups and saucers, teapot, water jug and the other articles in use as 'implements' (p.5). The complete phrase, 'the implements of the little feast', is much shorter than a list of all the things used, and, at the same time, surprisingly grand. The words convey the necessary information, but they also imply that afternoon tea is not to be dismissed as a casual snack to keep one going until the evening meal. It is a 'ceremony', a ritual custom, part of the traditional way of life which will seem quite foreign to Isabel Archer.

Chapter 21 gives a striking example of James's highly individual use of simple language. Towards the end of the chapter Isabel is thinking about her firm rejection of Caspar Goodwood. She reflects that she may eventually 'come to the end of the things that were not Caspar' (p.225).

It is remarkable how much meaning James achieves with these simple words. We know of Isabel's determination to see as much of life as she can. Here she admits that she may simply run out of things to discover. When she has seen the variety of the world she may find that nothing is, after all, as satisfactory—as steadfast and true—as Caspar. Weary of exploring, she may be glad to accept the restful security he offers her.

At the same time, these words define Isabel's attitude towards Caspar as completely negative. She may, one day, be grateful for his strong protection, but only after she has tried everything else. She would turn to Caspar only as a last resort.

James's simple vocabulary conveys all this meaning in a fraction of the space needed to analyse it.

Another habit of James's is to pile up phrases into long sentences which, at first, seem difficult to understand. This is a consequence of his wish to define things as accurately as possible. In Chapter 5, for example, James tells us that Ralph Touchett's time at the University of Oxford had made him 'English enough' in his outward manner:

> His outward conformity to the manners that surrounded him was none the less the mask of a mind that greatly enjoyed its independence, on which nothing long imposed itself, and, which, naturally inclined to adventure and irony, indulged in a boundless liberty of appreciation (p.38).

The basic meaning is simple: the American Ralph adopted English manners in order to fit into English society. He conformed to the English way of life, but kept his independence of mind. Yet James tells us much more than this.

The sentence begins with Ralph's fitting in, his 'conformity'. It then qualifies this idea, telling us that Ralph's English manners were a 'mask', a disguise behind which his 'mind' remained independent. He has permitted English manners to be imposed on his behaviour, but manners are outward things. Mentally, Ralph is too much of an individual to conform to anything for long. Inwardly, he is neither American nor English—he is himself. While controlling his behaviour to accord with English ideas of good conduct, he risks daring thoughts ('adventure') and notices odd contradictions ('irony'). Above all, his mind recognises no limit to its right to be freely aware of the world ('boundless liberty of appreciation').

Beginning with the idea of 'conformity' (Ralph's manners), the sentence builds up to a climax in the idea of 'liberty' (Ralph's mind). By this arrangement of his sentence James conveys not only information about Ralph, but also a sense of a man who is socially polite and restrained, yet mentally independent and vigorous. James expresses all this without using a single extraordinary word.

On a first reading of *The Portrait of a Lady* you should not stop to analyse James's prose as we have done with the above sentence. The best way to approach a novel by James for the first time is to read it through, stopping only at the ends of sections or chapters. His style does demand a high level of concentration in the reader, but part of his achievement is that he communicates the sense of a character or situation as well as a quantity of fine detail. The sentence we have discussed communicates immediately the sense of Ralph's character by putting one aspect of his personality at the beginning and another, opposing aspect at the end.

Read first for the sense; then go back and study the detail.

Imagery

Throughout *The Portrait of a Lady* James uses images to enrich his meanings and stimulate our response to them. Images appeal to our senses, converting ideas into pictures, making states of mind or moral qualities solid and visual. They help us to grasp abstractions.

Freedom, for example, is an abstraction, but we can see it when Lilian Ludlow refers to Isabel as a 'free greyhound' (p.30). Henrietta's image of Isabel as 'the stricken deer' (p.501) gives a vividly contrasting picture of wounded freedom. When Isabel recoils from Lord Warburton's proposal in Chapter 12 she is likened to 'some wild caught creature in a vast cage' (p.108). The 'vast cage' is the '"splendid" security' of marriage to an English lord, which would imprison her free nature. Ralph reminds us of this image when he tells Isabel that she is 'caught' because marriage to Osmond will put her into a 'cage' (p.341). The restrictions her marriage imposes on Isabel and the hopelessness of her situation are summed up by the image of her life as 'a dark, narrow alley with a dead wall at the end' (p.424).

The city of London's autumnal charm is conveyed by the image of 'a coloured gem . . . wrapped in a dusty cloth' (p.139). The Countess Gemini's flustered and excited way of snatching at tantalising things said by the clear-headed Madame Merle is precisely indicated by the image of the Countess plunging 'into the latter's lucidity as a poodle splashes after a thrown stick' (p.257). The connection between Ralph Touchett's contented mind and decaying body is imaged in the observation that his 'serenity was but the array of wild flowers niched in his ruin' (p.41).

James uses houses as images to symbolise qualities. Mrs Touchett discovers Isabel in a house whose dullness indicates a dull life. The Osmond house is called 'The Black Rock Palace' (Palazzo Roccanera) and becomes, for Isabel, 'the house of darkness' (p.429). Chapter 1 gives a brief history of Gardencourt, making the point that the old house has been shaped gradually by four centuries to become the 'rich perfection' (p.54) Isabel Archer first visits on her arrival from America. Compared to Gardencourt, Osmond's villa seems an artificial place, contrived by its owner to project an image of his fastidious taste.

The image of the innocent girl in a house called 'Gardencourt' prompts us to think of the Garden of Eden before Satan, in the form of a serpent, tempted Eve and caused the Fall. Isabel at Gardencourt is an American Eve. That Osmond is the serpent, the very incarnation of evil, is made clear by the image that comes into Isabel's mind in Chapter 42: '. . . his egotism lay hidden like a serpent in a bank of flowers' (p.430). In her innocence Isabel saw only the 'flowers': now she sees Osmond as the devil who has tempted her and destroyed her 'Garden'. Caspar Goodwood echoes the satanic image of the serpent when he refers to Osmond as 'the deadliest of fiends' (p.588).

Sea imagery

The image of a person's life as a boat at sea occurs repeatedly throughout *The Portrait of a Lady*. Ralph tells his father that he wishes 'to put a little wind' in Isabel's 'sails' (p.182). The wind, of course, is Mr Touchett's bequest. Ironically, Isabel thinks in similar imagery when she looks back on her early tenderness for Osmond. She had regarded him as a 'sceptical voyager . . . looking seaward, yet not putting to sea'. With her money she 'would launch his boat for him' (p.427).

These two instances of the boat image highlight the similarity between Isabel and Ralph: she wishes to do for Osmond what Ralph does for her. Both are generous characters. We recognise, too, that the image of the boat is appropriate in the case of Isabel—she is an explorer, eager for new experience—but not in the case of Osmond. Although his past affair with Madame Merle suggests that he was once capable of passion, he is now too careful a man to risk 'putting to sea'.

The development of Isabel's attitude towards Caspar Goodwood is expressed by the different images he suggests to her. Early in the novel Isabel thinks of marriage to Goodwood as a refuge to shield her from the sea of experience if she should weary of exploration. The image of Goodwood as 'a clear and quiet harbour enclosed by a brave granite breakwater' (p.225) emphasises his steady honesty and protective strength. At this stage in the story Isabel finds Goodwood too stolid to consider marrying him, but his impetuous journeys to see her in Italy obviously impress her as signs of vitality as well as persistence. In Chapter 47 he is no longer a static, quiet 'harbour'; she now imagines him as a boat at sea, like herself, and thinks of her last meeting with him as 'a collision between vessels in broad daylight' (p.484). When Goodwood's passion finally threatens to drown Isabel's sense of herself, he becomes 'a rushing torrent' associated with the 'fathomless waters' of the sea itself (p.590).

Principal characters

Isabel Archer

From a dull house and a narrow life in America, James's heroine comes to Europe determined to explore life freely and 'to be as happy as possible' (p.49). Tall, dark and 'willowy' with silver-grey eyes, she seems equipped for success by her attractive appearance and her independence of mind. When Ralph Touchett persuades his father to make her rich, he does so by saying, 'She wishes to be free, and your bequest will make her free' (p.183). Isabel is an imaginative young woman and Ralph wants to give her the chance to meet the requirements of her imagination (p.183).

Isabel's 'general air of being someone in particular' (p.42) leads Ralph to expect too much of her. She is less capable of sound judgement than he realises and her imagination, though active, is inconsistent and capricious. While insisting that she wants to see life for herself (p.150), and choose her own fate (p.161), she exposes the romantic vagueness of her mind when she says: 'A swift carriage, of a dark night, rattling with four horses over roads that one can't see—that's my idea of happiness' (p.165). James sums up the ambiguity of her temperament when he observes: 'The love of knowledge coexisted in her mind with the finest capacity for ignorance' (p.199).

In particular, Ralph hopes to protect Isabel's freedom by making it unnecessary for her to marry for security. Ironically, it is marriage that deprives her of even the illusion of freedom. Her determination to choose for herself, allied to her 'capacity for ignorance', prevents her from heeding other people's opinions of the egotistical Gilbert Osmond. Dismissing their advice as prejudiced or uninformed, she soon discovers that her wedding vows have made her the prisoner of a man who hates her.

At the end of the novel, with the knowledge she has gained through suffering, Isabel achieves a deeper understanding of herself and of the meaning of freedom. Her return to Osmond is an assertion of her own moral strength. Flight from Osmond would proclaim her inability to deal with him and would concede victory to the evil he embodies. In returning to him, Isabel honours her 'tremendous vows' (p.540) of marriage, and declares herself equal to the contest that must ensue with a man who is a 'serpent' (p.540) of egotism.

Daniel Tracy Touchett

Isabel Archer's uncle came to England from the state of Vermont in the 1830s as the junior partner in a bank of which he gained control some ten years later. He settled contentedly in England, bought the house and estate of Gardencourt, yet retained his American character. The 'fast friendship' (p.55) which Isabel forms with him reflects well on her. The discerning old man is 'full of kindness' towards his niece and allows himself to be persuaded by his son, Ralph, to make her financially independent by leaving her a substantial fortune, despite his fear that she 'may fall a victim to the fortune-hunters' (p.186).

Lydia Touchett

Forthright, plain-faced, and selfish, Mrs Touchett lives in Florence, 'virtually separated' (p.22) from her husband. On a visit to America she finds her niece, Isabel, in the old house in Albany and offers to take her to Europe. She accepts Isabel's right to 'do everything she chooses' (p.44), but does try to dissuade her from marrying Osmond. 'There's nothing *of* him', she says (p.334).

Intimacy between Mrs Touchett and Isabel ceases after Isabel's marriage. They meet again when Isabel travels from Rome to Gardencourt to see the dying Ralph.

Mrs Touchett is both a device by which James brings Isabel to Europe, and an example of arid female independence.

Ralph Touchett

Educated at an American school, Harvard University and the University of Oxford, Isabel's cousin, Ralph, followed in his father's footsteps to a position in the English branch of the bank. Eighteen months later he contracted a disease of the lungs which has restricted him 'to mere spectatorship at the game of life' (p.148).

Ralph functions as a means by which James guides our sympathy for Isabel. As an 'apostle of freedom' (p.462), Ralph underestimates the dangers freedom holds for his inexperienced cousin, but he understands Isabel's need to make her own choices. After he has provided for her financial independence through Mr Touchett's will, his policy of non-interference in her affairs is a mark of respect for her as a self-determining individual. The combination in Ralph of generosity and intelligence establishes him as the character whose evaluation of Isabel most nearly resembles James's own.

It soon becomes clear that Ralph loves Isabel, although ill health prevents him from offering her marriage and he loves her 'without hope' (p.346) for himself. Instead, he provides her with the condition of freedom by persuading his father to leave her seventy thousand pounds. Isabel gives Ralph a motive for staying alive in order to see what she does with her freedom. In Chapter 39 James defines 'the key to the mystery' of the ailing Ralph's continued existence: 'What kept Ralph alive was simply the fact that he had not yet seen enough of the person in the world in whom he was most interested' (p.395).

When it becomes apparent that Isabel has lost her freedom, Ralph dies. Ralph is, therefore, even more dependent on Isabel's freedom than Osmond is on her submission and her money. The essential difference between the two men in relation to Isabel is that Ralph's imagination requires her to be free to express herself, while Osmond requires her to express only him.

Lord Warburton

Isabel's English suitor is thirty-five, handsome, and charming—a fine 'specimen of an English gentleman' (p.65). A close friend of Ralph Touchett, he often visits Gardencourt from his neighbouring estate, Lockleigh. He falls in love with Isabel 'at first sight' (p.104) and when he proposes marriage to her, offers to live wherever she may choose. Warburton's high position, his generosity, and the humanitarian political views that show him to be 'a nobleman of the newest pattern' (p.69) make Isabel's rejection of him especially significant.

Warburton is at once the ideal figure that Isabel's reading of novels has led her to expect among the English aristocracy, and a precisely drawn individual character of great personal appeal. In addition to being 'well-made' (p.7), he is courteous, ardent, self-disciplined, and genuinely concerned about the inequalities of the English social system, despite his own privileged position within it. Isabel's inability to fall in love with so attractive and complete a man is a measure of the regard she has for her own idea of freedom. Warburton's withdrawal from courting Pansy when he realises the girl prefers Rosier, demonstrates his consideration of others. His proposal, which offers freedom within marriage, is Isabel's most 'splendid' (p.108) lost opportunity.

Caspar Goodwood

Thoroughly American both in background and manner, Goodwood is a complete contrast to Isabel's other rejected suitor, Lord Warburton. Goodwood, the businessman, is a conservative; Warburton, the aristocrat, is a radical. Warburton treats Isabel with unfailing courtesy; Goodwood's manner is aggressive.

After an education at Harvard University, Goodwood became manager of his father's cotton factory in Boston. (Osmond thinks of him as 'a perpendicular Bostonian', p.494). His honest, solid nature is expressed in his name: 'Good-wood'. His resolute character shows in a physical appearance which Isabel finds disagreeably angular and rigid: 'His jaw was too square and set and his figure too straight and stiff' (p.116). He lacks expressiveness and looks at the world out of 'blue eyes of remarkable fixedness' (p.36). Although he is 'the finest young man she had ever seen' (p.36) before her departure from America, Isabel is not at any time in love with Goodwood. At best he might afford her a refuge from the world if she should tire of exploring, but she feels his persistence as a threat to her freedom, and accordingly treats him harshly.

In the last chapter, when Goodwood beseeches Isabel to leave Osmond and turn to him, she is greatly moved by his passion. Although she feels, at last, the full force of his love for her—his kiss is like 'white lightning' (p.591)—she chooses not to be rescued from the consequences of her marriage and her promise to Pansy Osmond. Goodwood admits to Isabel that he is 'selfish as iron' (p.332). To be rescued by someone of such 'intense identity' (p.591) would mean the loss of her own.

Henrietta Stackpole

Isabel thinks of Henrietta as a 'model' of 'useful activity' (p.52) and female independence (p.53). Henrietta is to be admired for supporting the three children of her infirm, widowed sister and paying their school bills out of her earnings as a journalist for a New York journal, the

Interviewer. Our early impressions are of a brash and prejudiced young American patriot who expresses contempt for the past and the British way of life before she has taken the trouble to understand either. Her 'clear-cut views' are shallow, and her tactless manner provokes Isabel to say, 'My poor Henrietta, you've no sense of privacy' (p.87). If Mrs Touchett represents female independence at its most arid, Henrietta exemplifies the same condition at its most strident.

Yet Henrietta develops with the novel. She angers Isabel by her encouragement of Goodwood, but her friendship is firm and lasting. 'I love you intensely, Isabel', she says in Chapter 17 (p.166). She is perceptive enough to see the danger inherent in Isabel's sudden wealth, and warns her that her money will confine her 'to the society of a few selfish and heartless people' who will exploit her tendency to take 'romantic views' (p.217).

Human feeling triumphs over prejudice when Henrietta accompanies the ailing Ralph on his journey home from Rome; and her mellowing is completed by her engagement to Mr Bantling.

Serena Merle

Madame Merle's name contains a warning. 'Merle' is the French word for 'blackbird' and implies cunning. 'A woman of strong impulses kept in admirable order' (p.175), Madame Merle seems at first to embody Isabel's ideal of individual freedom. Charming and sophisticated, her accomplishments in music, painting and needlework, her polished manners, handsome bearing, freedom of movement and independence of mind, all suggest a woman who has chosen to be exactly as she is. 'I should awfully like to be *so*!' Isabel thinks (p.189), and her admiration is unaffected by the fact that Madame Merle is not the European she seems, but was born in the Brooklyn navy-yard, the daughter of a US navy officer.

Isabel cannot accept Madame Merle's opinion that a person's character is always expressed by 'an envelope of circumstances' or a 'cluster of appurtenances' (p.201), such as his or her clothes, house, possessions, choice of books and friends. Isabel disagrees: her true self is not defined by such outward things. Ironically, Isabel is defined by the crucial circumstance of being rich when Osmond marries her for her money. Isabel's illusions end in Chapter 51 when she learns from the Countess Gemini that Madame Merle had arranged the marriage and that Pansy is Madame Merle's illegitimate daughter by Osmond.

Madame Merle has some of the qualities of a tragic figure. Her deep falsity in betraying Isabel brings her no happiness. She suffers remorse for sacrificing Isabel to Osmond. The rewards of her scheming are Osmond's undisguised contempt (pp.520–5) and Pansy's dislike (p.557).

The futility of her life is summed up in her anguished cry to Osmond: 'Have I been so vile all for nothing?' (p.525). Her former lover has dried up her soul (p.522).

Gilbert Osmond

Prematurely grey at forty, Osmond's obsession with appearances is indicated by his own. His beard, 'cut in the manner of the portraits of the sixteenth century and surmounted by a fair moustache', suggests a preoccupation with 'style' (p.228). This is the key to a character concerned above all with his own image as a connoisseur.

Ralph warns Isabel to beware, remarking sardonically that Osmond 'has a great dread of vulgarity; that's his special line; he hasn't any other that I know of' (p.249), but Isabel is captivated by Osmond's pose. She interprets his fastidious taste and apparent indifference to worldly matters as sure signs of a noble character. Ralph angers her by calling Osmond 'a sterile dilettante' (p.345). She marries Osmond because she has fallen in love with him, believes he loves her, and because she sees in his lack of money the opportunity to be generous with hers. After a year or two of marriage the antagonism between Osmond and Isabel is the inevitable opposition of a mean spirit to a generous one.

Osmond's true character is revealed by his cold exploitation of Madame Merle and his treatment of Pansy, whom he brings up 'in the old way' (p.353) to submit to his wishes in everything. He regards her as 'a precious work of art' (p.532), a possession, and suppresses her development in order to retain control of her.

Isabel, too, seems reduced to the status of an object in Osmond's collection, until she defies him by visiting Ralph, and then returning to face the consequences of her rebellion.

Pansy Osmond

The illegitimate daughter of Gilbert Osmond and Madame Merle, Pansy is completely dominated by her father who calls her his 'little saint of heaven' and his 'great happiness' (p.266) because he has designed her himself. Isabel likens her to 'a sheet of blank paper' (p.278), which suggests emptiness as well as innocence. Mrs Touchett calls her 'an uncanny child' (p.274) because it is extraordinary that someone nearly sixteen years old should be so unformed. Pansy's unfashionable white dress reflects Osmond's refusal to let her mature naturally. She confesses to Isabel that she is 'too young to think about marriage' (p.316), but Osmond has so prevented her from developing as an individual that she is almost incapable of thinking about anything.

Pansy's one show of resistance to Osmond is her loyalty to Edward

Rosier and her refusal to like Lord Warburton to order. Osmond crushes this slight defiance by sending her away to the loneliness and solemnity of the convent. Visiting her in Chapter 52, Isabel realises that she has 'bowed her pretty head to authority' (p.557). Pansy's appeal to Isabel to return does suggest, however, that she sees her step-mother as a source of help. As she tells Rosier of Isabel in Chapter 38, 'She's not afraid of anyone' (p.387).

Countess Gemini

Gilbert Osmond's sister, Amy, represents the immoral realities of Florentine society which, Isabel realises, account for many of the 'traditions' Osmond reveres (p.432). The Countess is married to a dull, impoverished and unpopular Tuscan count who gambles too much and to whom she is reputed to be frequently unfaithful. Thin-lipped and bird-like, she is an odd, superficial woman of no beauty but 'high fashion', with 'a great deal of manner' (p.254).

The Countess can be 'unpleasantly perverse' (p.500), as in her interpretation of Pansy's response to Lord Warburton; but a genuine liking for Isabel, as well as resentment of Osmond, motivates her revelation in Chapter 51 of Pansy's parentage and the conspiracy between Osmond and Madame Merle.

Edward Rosier

A native of New York, 'Ned' Rosier lives in Paris where he was brought up by his father, an old friend of the late Mr Archer. Isabel had met Rosier first in France when they were both children.

Like Osmond, Rosier is a connoisseur and collector of fine things. Even when he falls in love with Pansy he thinks of her as an object, 'a consummate piece' (p.357) like the figure of a shepherdess made of Dresden china. Unlike Osmond, Rosier is capable of change: he sells nearly all his treasured possessions in the hope of becoming rich enough to be accepted by Osmond as a husband for Pansy. The sacrifice of his *bibelots* (precious artistic objects) fails to win Osmond's approval, but redeems Rosier's character.

Minor characters

Lilian Ludlow

Eldest and plainest of the Archer sisters, she is 'usually thought the most sensible' of the three (p.30). She watches Isabel 'as a motherly spaniel might watch a free greyhound' and wishes 'to see her safely married' (p.30). She visits Isabel in Europe, stays for five months, and tries, unsuccessfully, to persuade her to return to America.

Edith Keyes

The second of the Archer girls, she is the 'beauty' among them (p.30). Married to an officer of the United States Engineers, she is mentioned briefly in Chapter 4 but does not appear in the novel in person.

Edmund Ludlow

Isabel's brother-in-law by his marriage to Lilian. A lawyer, he is 'a young man with a loud voice and an enthusiasm for his profession' (p.30).

The Misses Molyneux

Lord Warburton's two unmarried sisters who live with him at Lockleigh in 'a wilderness of faded chintz' (p.76). 'Quiet and reasonable and satisfied', they revere their brother without understanding him. Though 'capable of deep emotion', they display 'a want of play of mind' (p.76) and exactly represent the kind of woman Isabel does not wish to be.

Robert Bantling

A friend of Ralph Touchett, Mr Bantling is a stout, sleek, smiling man of forty. On terms of 'great personal intimacy' (p.217), he escorts Henrietta on her travels in Europe, visits her in America, and becomes engaged to her near the end of the novel.

Sir Matthew Hope

An eminent London physician who attends both Mr Touchett and Ralph in their final illnesses. Ralph dislikes him, preferring the local doctor, and pretends to be dead in order to be rid of his attentions.

Mother Catherine

The kindly nun who is in charge of Pansy's convent.

Mr and Mrs Luce

American friends of Mrs Touchett who lead aimless lives of luxury in Paris.

Hints for study

PART 4 OF THESE NOTES now suggests ways in which you should work on your own, and aims to help you prepare answers to various questions which you may be asked. The first section provides a list of topics for study, and for each topic you might (a) prepare your own list of the points which you could make in an answer, and (b) select relevant quotations. You will sometimes find it useful to organise your points under subheadings, and you might think about the best order in which you could deal with your points, although the particular phrasing of the questions will influence this aspect of your answer. The second section provides some useful useful quotations, and the third section shows how various points can be organised into essay answers. Finally, the fourth section gives four model answers to specimen questions. It will be a useful exercise to alter and expand these answers to accord with your own opinions. Practice organising your points and write your own answers to the topics suggested.

Topics to select for detailed study

1. The major characters: (a) Isabel Archer (b) Ralph Touchett (c) Madame Merle (d) Gilbert Osmond (e) Lord Warburton (f) Caspar Goodwood.
2. Isabel's refusal of Lord Warburton and Caspar Goodwood.
3. The significance of references to art and architecture (many are listed in the 'Notes and Glossary' sections in Part 2).
4. The discrepancy between Isabel's awareness and the reader's.
5. The role and effectiveness of imagery.
6. James's language.
7. The technique of the single 'lighted figure'.
8. James's view of female independence in: (a) Isabel (b) Mrs Touchett (c) Henrietta Stackpole (d) Madame Merle.
9. The roles of: (a) Pansy Osmond (b) Edward Rosier (c) the Countess Gemini.
10. James's view of the American character.
11. James's view of marriage.
12. The theme of egotism.

Selected quotations

Isabel Archer

''"Oh, I hoped there would be a lord; it's just like a novel!"'' (p.17).

'Her imagination was by habit ridiculously active; when the door was not open it jumped out of the window' (p.32).

'It often seemed to her that she thought too much about herself; you could have made her colour, any day in the year, by calling her a rank egoist' (p.53).

'She was too young, too impatient to live, too unacquainted with pain' (p.54).

''"No, I don't wish to touch the cup of experience. It's a poisoned drink! I only want to see for myself"'' (p.150).

''". . . I wish to choose my fate"'' (p.161).

''"A swift carriage, of a dark night, rattling with four horses over roads that one can't see—that's my idea of happiness"'' (p.165).

''"She's not afraid of anyone"'' (p.387).

'Very often, however, she felt afraid . . .' (p.433).

'She might have had another life and she might have been a woman more blest' (p.569).

Daniel Tracy Touchett

'. . . a shrewd American banker' (p.6).

''"Daddy's very fond of pleasure—of other people's"'' (p.11).

''"I've always ascertained for myself—got my information in the natural form. I never asked many questions even; I just kept quiet and took notice"'' (p.56).

Lydia Touchett

'She was a plain-faced old woman, without graces and without any great elegance, but with an extreme respect for her own motives' (p.22).

''"My point of view, thank God, is personal"'' (p.60).

Ralph Touchett

'Living as he now lived was like reading a good book in translation—a meagre entertainment for a young man who felt that he might have been an excellent linguist' (p.40).

'. . . the imagination of loving—as distinguished from that of being loved—had still a place in his reduced sketch' (p.41).

'"I shall get just the good I said a few moments ago I wished to put into Isabel's reach—that of having met the requirements of my imagination"' (p.186).

'What kept Ralph alive was simply the fact that he had not yet seen enough of the person in the world in whom he was most interested: he was not yet satisfied' (p.395).

'There was something in Ralph's talk, in his smile, in the mere fact of his being in Rome, that made the blasted circle round which she walked more spacious. He made her feel the good of the world; he made her feel what might have been' (p.434).

'"I believe I ruined you", he wailed' (p.576).

Lord Warburton

'A specimen of an English gentleman' (p.65).

'. . . Isabel gathered that Lord Warburton was a nobleman of the newest pattern, a reformer, a radical, a contemner of ancient ways' (p.69).

'"I don't make mistakes about such things; I'm a very judicious animal. I don't go off easily, but when I'm touched, it's for life"' (p.105).

'He might have been addressing a small committee—making all quietly and clearly a statement of importance; aided by an occasional look at a paper of notes concealed in his hat, which he had not again put on' (p.292).

Caspar Goodwood

'There was a disagreeably strong push, a kind of hardness of presence, in his way of rising before her' (p.114).

'His jaw was too square and set and his figure too straight and stiff: these things suggested a want of easy consonance with the deeper rhythms of life' (p.116).

'It was conceivable that these impediments should some day prove a sort of blessing in disguise—a clear and quiet harbour enclosed by a brave granite breakwater' (p.225).

'"I'm selfish as iron"' (p.332).

Henrietta Stackpole

'Henrietta, for Isabel, was chiefly a proof that a woman might suffice to herself and be happy' (p.53).

'"She's too personal—considering that she expects other people not to be. She walks in without knocking at the door"' (p.93).

Serena Merle

'She was in a word a woman of strong impulses kept in admirable order. This commended itself to Isabel as an ideal combination' (p.175).

'"When you've lived as long as I you'll see that every human being has his shell and that you must take the shell into account. By the shell I mean the whole envelope of circumstances. There's no such thing as an isolated man or woman; we're each of us made up of some cluster of appurtenances"' (p.201).

'Her conception of human motives might, in certain lights, have been acquired at the court of some kingdom in decadence, and there were several in her list of which our heroine had not even heard' (p.324).

'"Have I been so vile all for nothing?"' (p.525).

Gilbert Osmond

'He had consulted his taste in everything—his taste alone perhaps, as a sick man consciously incurable consults at last only his lawyer: that was what made him so different from everyone else' (p.262).

'"No, I'm not conventional: I'm convention itself"' (p.312).

'"He's not important—no, he's not important; he's a man to whom importance is supremely indifferent"' (p.346).

'He took himself so seriously; it was something appalling. Under all his culture, his cleverness, his amenity, under his good-nature, his facility, his knowledge of life, his egotism lay hidden like a serpent in a bank of flowers' (pp.429–30).

Pansy Osmond

'Pansy was really a blank page, a pure white surface, successfully kept so; she had neither art, nor guile, nor temper, nor talent—only two or three small exquisite instincts: for knowing a friend, for avoiding a mistake, for taking care of an old toy or a new frock' (p.315).

Countess Gemini

'. . . to a casual view the Countess Gemini revealed no depths' (p.254).

'"I never congratulate any girl on marrying; I think they ought to make it somehow not quite so awful a steel trap"' (p.356).

'"I'm thought a great scatterbrain, but I've had enough application of mind to follow up those two"' (p.546).

Edward Rosier

'"You think I ought to do something, and so do I, so long as you leave it vague"' (p.215).
'"Ah, my dear lady, pity me!"' (p.528).

Arranging material to answer questions

The role of Madame Merle

Madame Merle performs two functions: (1) Isabel's development in awareness is reflected in a changing attitude towards her, and (2) she is a device by which James constructs the trap in which Isabel is caught. Bear these points in mind when selecting your material which should include:

(a) Isabel's first impressions of her as 'a great lady' (p.190) in Chapters 18 and 19; the warnings implicit in Ralph's comments (pp.176–7, 250–2), and in Madame Merle's statement to Isabel that 'he doesn't like me' (p.198).

(b) the reader's first impression of her, as distinct from Isabel's; the reader's reaction to her assumption that Isabel has been mercenary towards Mr Touchett (p.208); the widening gap between the reader's and Isabel's perception of her.

(c) incidents which develop the reader's perception, like the conversations she has with Osmond in Chapter 22, with Countess Gemini in Chapter 25, with Osmond in Chapters 26 and 49.

(d) the gradual alignment of Isabel's view with the reader's as she thinks about Madame Merle in Chapters 31, 40, and at the end of Chapter 42; the meeting with Isabel in Chapter 49 compared to the final confrontation in Chapter 52 after the Countess's revelations in Chapter 51.

The view of marriage deducible from the novel

(a) Evaluate the marriages which are displayed or referred to:
1 Mr and Mrs Touchett
2 Isabel Archer's sisters
3 Lord Warburton's reference to 'English wives' (p.70)
4 Mr and Mrs Luce (Chapter 20)
5 Count and Countess Gemini
6 Mr and Mrs Gilbert Osmond.

(b) Assess James's view of female independence in:
1 Henrietta Stackpole
2 Madame Merle
3 Mrs Touchett
4 Isabel before her marriage.
(c) What attitudes towards marriage do you find in Lord Warburton, Caspar Goodwood and Edward Rosier?
(d) What is the significance of Henrietta's engagement to Mr Bantling?

The crucial stages of Isabel Archer's progress from innocence to experience

(a) Define the principal qualities of Isabel's character when she arrives at Gardencourt.
(b) Illustrate her determination to protect her freedom, referring to her reasons for refusing Warburton and Goodwood.
(c) Critically analyse her reasons for marrying Gilbert Osmond.
(d) Assess Isabel's awareness of her situation as revealed in Chapter 42.
(e) Assess the impact of the Countess's revelations in Chapter 51.
(f) Compare her choice at the end of the novel to earlier choices she has made.

The significance of James's settings

See the notes on the significance of houses in general, and Gardencourt in particular, in the section on imagery in Part 3. Discuss James's use of the following settings:
(a) Gardencourt in Chapters 1, 5, 53–5
(b) The old Albany house in Chapter 3
(c) Lockleigh in Chapter 8
(d) Paris in Chapter 20
(e) Osmond's villa near Florence in Chapters 22 and 24
(f) Florence in Chapter 23
(g) Rome, especially St Peter's basilica in Chapter 27, the Palazzo Roccanera in Chapter 36, the ruins in Chapter 49, and Coliseum in Chapter 50.

The theme of egotism

Consider this topic as it might be presented in a question: 'Gilbert Osmond is the villain of the novel and Madame Merle is his accomplice, but their selfishness is different only in degree from that of the other characters. With the exception of old Mr Touchett, everyone seeks to exploit Isabel Archer. Discuss.'

This question challenges your convictions about the interpretation of the novel which has been developed throughout these notes. You have become accustomed to thinking of Ralph as generous, Mrs Touchett as eccentric but fundamentally decent, Henrietta as brash but affectionate, the Countess Gemini as gossipy and immoral but fond of Isabel. The falsity of Osmond and Madame Merle in exploiting Isabel sets them apart as the two wickedly selfish characters in James's cast.

Now consider and respond to the following suggestions, looking in the novel for evidence either to refute or to justify them:

(a) Mrs Touchett's motive in taking Isabel to Europe is selfish: she wants Isabel to do her 'credit' (p.43).

(b) Ralph appears to be generous towards Isabel, but admits his selfishness when he tells Mr Touchett that her freedom will enable him to meet the 'requirements' of his imagination (p.186).

(c) Henrietta selfishly wants Isabel to marry Goodwood in order to satisfy her own American prejudices.

(d) Both Pansy Osmond and Edward Rosier are interested in Isabel only because they think she can help them.

(e) The Countess Gemini reveals the truth about Osmond, Madame Merle and Pansy not out of kindness to Isabel, but as an act of revenge for Osmond's humiliating treatment of herself, and because she hates Madame Merle.

(f) Both Warburton and Goodwood want Isabel for a wife. To this extent they, too, are selfish in their relation to her.

Specimen questions and model answers

Of all her suitors, why does Isabel Archer choose to marry Gilbert Osmond?

Although Caspar Goodwood is a forceful and dependable man, genuinely in love with Isabel, we are not surprised when she rejects him. The manager of a Boston cotton factory, square of jaw and drab of dress, cannot fulfil the requirements of an imagination like Isabel's. She is too romantic to be in love with him, too eager for knowledge of life to settle into the dull security of the limited life he seems to offer. 'Selfish as iron' (p.332), Goodwood has an 'intense identity' (p.591) which constitutes a threat to Isabel's self-possession. Marriage to someone so rigid and provincial would mean surrendering her power to choose her own fate before she has had an opportunity to discover what other possibilities life may hold.

Her English suitor, Lord Warburton, seems more likely to succeed. A lord is a romantic figure to Isabel. 'It's just like a novel,' she says when she first meets him (p.17). Warburton is an interesting and attractive man—'he had an excellent manner with women' (p.19)—with a fine estate and an important position in society. Isabel cannot marry him, however, because, as Lady Warburton, she would feel confined by the social system he represents, in spite of his radical political views. Marriage to an English aristocrat would oblige her to behave like one herself, and put an end to her free exploration of life.

Isabel is aware that Goodwood and Warburton are both good men. She admires Goodwood's honesty and strength of character. She likes Lord Warburton and realises that nineteen women out of twenty would have been happy to marry him. James shows Isabel unable to fall in love with such a man in order to emphasise her firm determination to remain in command of herself.

The appeal of Gilbert Osmond is that he seems to live freely, according to his own exacting standards, and detached from all worldly considerations. His only visible relationship is to his daughter, Pansy. He seems to Isabel to be detached even from the artistic objects with which he has furnished his house near Florence, and to live for his perceptions of things rather than for the things themselves. He does not seem to care that he has 'no property, no title, no honours, no houses, no lands, nor position, nor reputation, nor brilliant belongings of any sort' (p.347). Isabel proudly tells Ralph that it is the absence of these things that pleases her. Isabel chooses to marry a man who, she believes, has refused to be defined by anything outside his own noble character. He seems 'a specimen apart' (p.261), an original.

Osmond is, of course, nothing of the kind. There is nothing original about marrying for money. In her innocence Isabel confuses appearance with reality and makes a tragic mistake.

Illustrate James's use of the discrepancy between Isabel's awareness and the reader's

---

Chapter 21 informs the reader that Isabel sometimes thinks of Warburton and Goodwood. She considers that Warburton will get over his disappointment, but not Goodwood. At this stage in her progress she looks forward to Italy as 'a land of promise' (p.223), yet reflects that one day she may tire of exploring and be grateful for the peace and protection Goodwood offers (p.225). Immediately after this, in Chapter 22, the scene shifts to Gilbert Osmond's house just outside Florence as James takes the reader to Italy ahead of Isabel, to see what awaits her there. It is at once evident that Osmond is a cold, conceited man who dominates his daughter and is on suspiciously familiar terms with Madame Merle. When Madame Merle tells Osmond that she wants him to marry Isabel (p.243), Isabel's 'land of promise' is revealed as dangerous country. The reader is prompted to wonder how soon it may be before Isabel discovers Madame Merle's double-dealing and comes to regret her refusal of Goodwood's strong security and loyal, honest heart.

James significantly widens the gap between Isabel's and the reader's knowledge of affairs in Chapters 25, 26 and 35. In Chapter 25, while Osmond is being charming to Isabel, James allows the reader to over-hear the conversation between the Countess Gemini and Madame Merle in which the Countess makes the alarming suggestion that Isabel is about to be 'sacrificed' (p.273). The reader's concern for Isabel's safety increases in Chapter 26 when Osmond, chillingly, uses the same word (p.286). In Chapter 35, while Isabel is thinking of Osmond as 'her lover, her own' (p.352), Osmond regards her not as a person but as an object of 'decorative value' (p.350). While Isabel thinks she is loved for herself, the reader is made aware that Osmond looks upon her as a 'silver plate' on which he may 'heap up' his own egotism for elegant display. This discrepancy between Isabel's view of things and the reader's maintains the suspense of the novel until Chapter 42, when Isabel sits up until the small hours of the morning, facing the fact that her husband is a 'serpent' of egotism (p.430) and that her marriage to him is 'horrible' (p.433).

From Chapter 42 to the end of the novel the suspense is of a different kind. There is still a gap between Isabel's knowledge and the reader's. Isabel still has to learn the truth about Osmond and Madame Merle's manipulation of her, and Pansy's parentage has yet to be revealed. Since Chapter 22 the reader has been in a better position than Isabel to suspect the truth of Madame Merle's relation to Pansy. As the gap in awareness closes in the last part of the novel, however, the main interest is not so much in what Isabel will find out about her situation as in how she will act, now that her innocence has been replaced by bitter experience and her dream of freedom has faded.

What is Henry James's view of the American character?

Half-jokingly, Lord Warburton tells Isabel that of all the people in the world, Americans are the most 'grossly superstitious' and 'conservative' (p.69). That James's view of the American character is more complex than this is reflected by the range of people he invents for the novel. If the worst of them are Americans, so are the best.

Accusing Isabel of 'a patriotism so heated that it scorched' (p.60), Ralph calls her 'Columbia' and draws a caricature of her in which she is represented 'as a very pretty young woman dressed, on the lines of the prevailing fashion, in the folds of the national banner' (p.61). Ralph's view of Isabel is so close to the author's that we may suppose James, too, regarded his heroine's qualities as American in type. Isabel is innocent, enthusiastic and determined. She is also pretty, and we are clearly intended to like her. At the same time, James directs our attention to her faults. 'Probably very liable to the sin of self-esteem' (p.50), she is limited by her romantic view of life. For her the American Civil War is a heroic tale of valour on both sides, instead of a bitter, bloody struggle between fellow countrymen (p.35). Although she has 'a certain nobleness of imagination' (p.51), her thoughts are 'a tangle of vague outlines' (p.50). 'Fond of her own way,' as Mrs Touchett says (p.29), her determination to choose for herself closes her mind to the opinions of others. Yet James carefully preserves our sympathy for Isabel and shows her eventually rising above the unhappiness she has, largely, brought upon herself. Her final act of choice—to return to Osmond and Pansy—is a mature one, made in full knowledge of its implications. We must, in the end, admire Isabel.

The Touchetts are a mixed group. Mrs Touchett is eccentric and selfish, but Mr Touchett has achieved success as a banker and wisdom as a human being. The loving yet unsentimental relationship between him and Ralph is one of the most affecting elements of the story. Ralph himself might appear to be less of an American than either of his parents, but James makes it clear that while the University of Oxford has supplied him with English manners, his mind remains as independent as it always was. Ralph is the most generous and intelligent person in James's cast of characters. If the Touchetts fail to be a model American family, there is much to be commended in the father and the son.

The most strident of James's Americans is Henrietta Stackpole. Her disregard for the privacy of others, her open contempt for the past and the British way of life even when she is in the company of the courteous Lord Warburton, are comic to the point of caricature. Yet her affection for Isabel is firm; she learns to care for Ralph to accompany him home from Rome; and she mellows into the future Mrs Bantling.

The most uncompromisingly American character is Caspar Goodwood, with his energy, his faith in persistence, and his dislike of England and Europe. His fidelity is admirable, but his refusal to accept that Isabel does not love him prevents us from according him our sympathy. In Goodwood Henry James associates American dynamism both with passion and with insensitivity.

The villainous Gilbert Osmond and his accomplice, Madame Merle, are both 'vague' (p.249) Americans. This suggests that Americans can learn to be as devious and immoral as anyone, especially with Europe as their sphere of operation.

It may be deduced from the novel's principal characters that James admires the kind of American energy that made Mr Touchett successful, but deplores the American brashness of Henrietta. He is aware that youthful American idealism is likely to be out of its depth among the sophistications of Europe. Independence of mind based on experience and intellect, as in Ralph, is good; but the American combination of innocence and determination, as in Isabel, is a recipe for unhappiness. The happiest Americans—perhaps the best—seem to be those expatriates who choose to settle in England, like Mr Touchett, Ralph, or Henry James himself.

Interpret the ending of *The Portrait of a Lady*

James's achievement in the last part of *The Portrait of a Lady* is to turn Isabel's defeat into victory. At the end of the nineteenth century it was much more difficult for a woman to leave her husband than it is today in western society, despite Henrietta's observation to Isabel that 'nothis more common in our Western cities' (p.502). Divorce still meant disgrace. Yet it is not fear of public disgrace that causes Isabel to reject Caspar Goodwood's passionate attempt to rescue her in the last chapter.

In Chapter 51, during the argument about Isabel's going to see the dying Ralph, Osmond says: '. . . I think we should accept the consequences of our actions, and what I value most in life is the honour of a thing!' (p.537). Isabel accepts the truth of this, even though it is said by the false Osmond. The consequence of her marriage is that she is bound to Osmond as his wife. The consequence of her promise to Pansy in Chapter 52 is an obligation to return to Rome. She could leave Osmond and break her promise to Pansy; instead, she chooses the way of 'honour' and duty. The main point here is the element of choice.

During Warburton's last visit to Rome, and throughout his attentions to Pansy, it is clear that he still loves Isabel and would help her if she would let him. James brings Warburton and then Goodwood back into Isabel's life in order to make it clear that assistance and escape are available to her. She need not remain Osmond's prisoner. In returning to Osmond at the end, Isabel chooses honour; she does not have it thrust upon her.

Isabel disagrees with Madame Merle's opinion in Chapter 19 that everyone is made up of an 'envelope of circumstances' (p.201), because this means that no one is really free. Isabel cannot accept that people are always determined by the circumstances of their lives irrespective of their individual wills. To go away with Goodwood would imply that Madame Merle was right after all. It would be an admission by Isabel that the 'envelope' of her unhappy circumstances was powerful enough to make her run away from the consequences of her own actions with a man she has never loved.

The decision to return to Rome must, therefore, be seen as a further refutation of Madame Merle's view and as the greatest expression of

Isabel's freedom. It marks her triumph over her circumstances and over the immature ideal of freedom she brought with her from America. That ideal had equated freedom with liberty of appreciation and self-fulfilment, yet it led her into marrying a man who seeks to extinguish her. It is not enough 'to be free to follow out a good feeling' (p.346). Freedom now means being in a position to choose the right thing with reference to all the circumstances, all the responsibilities, and in full awareness of probable consequences. In choosing to go back, Isabel rises above her circumstances, keeps her promises, and freely accepts responsibility for her own past and her own future.

Part 5

Suggestions for further reading

The text

The Portrait of a Lady, Penguin Books, Harmondsworth, 1963; reprinted with preface, 1966; 15th reprinting of text with preface, 1979.
The edition used in these notes.

The Portrait of a Lady, with an introduction by Leon Edel, Riverside
Editions, Houghton Mifflin Co., Boston, 1956. Useful introduction
by James's biographer.

Other works by Henry James

The American, Signet Books, New American Library, New York,
undated. *Roderick Hudson*; *The Europeans*; *Washington Square*; *The
Bostonians*; *The Princess Casamassima*; *The Aspern Papers*; *The Turn
of the Screw and other Stories*; *The Wings of the Dove*, all currently
available in paperback editions by Penguin Books, Harmondsworth.

The Art of the Novel. Critical Prefaces by Henry James, with introduc-
tion by R.P. Blackmur, Charles Scribner's Sons, New York, 1934.
James's reflections on his craft in the prefaces written for the 'New
York' edition of his works.

The House of Fiction, edited with an introduction by Leon Edel, Rupert
Hart-Davis, London, 1957. Includes some of James's most famous
critical essays, including 'The Art of Fiction', 'The Great Form', and
several reviews of work by writers of his time.

The Notebooks of Henry James, edited by F.O. Matthiessen and
Kenneth B. Murdock, Oxford University Press, New York, 1947;
reprinted as a Galaxy Book, 1961. The notes James made as he
worked on ideas for his stories. Pages 15–19 refer particularly to the
composition of *The Portrait of a Lady*.

General reading

ANDERSON, QUENTIN: *The American Henry James*, Rutgers University
Press, New Brunswick, 1957. Examines James's specifically American
qualities.

BEACH, JOSEPH WARREN: *The Method of Henry James*, Yale University Press, New Haven, 1918. Still an invaluable study of James's style.

CARGILL, OSCAR: *The Novels of Henry James*, Macmillan, New York, 1961. An indispensable handbook for the serious Jamesian scholar. Cargill refers widely to other critics' readings and makes his own judgements. Pages 78–119 discuss *The Portrait of a Lady*.

EDEL, LEON: *The Life of Henry James*, Rupert Hart-Davis, London, 1953–72, five volumes; reprinted in two volumes by Penguin Books, Harmondsworth, 1977. The definitive biography.

———(ED.): *Henry James. Twentieth-Century Views*, Prentice-Hall, Englewood Cliffs, New Jersey, 1963. A collection of critical essays ranging from early reactions to James by Joseph Conrad, Max Beerbohm and Ezra Pound, to more recent assessments by Irving Howe and Leon Edel.

JEFFERSON, D.W.: *Henry James*, Writers and Critics series, Oliver and Boyd, Edinburgh and London, 1960; and Grove Press, New York, 1961. A compact but substantial survey of James's work, containing a useful discussion of Isabel Archer as a typical American girl.

KROOK, DOROTHEA: *The Ordeal of Consciousness in Henry James*, Cambridge University Press, Cambridge, 1962. Chapter 2 discusses the development of Isabel Archer's consciousness.

LEAVIS, F.R.: *The Great Tradition*, Chatto and Windus, London, 1948; and George W. Stewart, New York, 1950. Chapter 3 is a famous, idiosyncratic essay on James's fiction. Leavis considers *The Portrait of a Lady* and *The Bostonians* 'the two most brilliant novels in the language'.

MATTHIESSEN, F.O.: *Henry James: The Major Phase*, Oxford University Press, New York, 1944; reprinted as a Galaxy Book, 1963. The last chapter discusses James's revisions of *The Portrait of a Lady*.

PUTT, S. GORLEY: *A Reader's Guide to Henry James*, Thames and Hudson, 1966. An excellent commentary; not as rudimentary as its title suggests. *The Portrait of a Lady* is analysed at length in Chapter 5.

TANNER, TONY (ED.): *Henry James*, Modern Judgements series, Macmillan, London, 1968. A good selection of modern articles on James. The essay by J.H. Raleigh, 'Henry James: The Poetics of Empiricism' (pp.52–70), is especially relevant to the themes of perception and taste in *The Portrait of a Lady*.

The author of these notes

MARSHALL WALKER obtained his M.A. and Ph.D. degrees from the University of Glasgow. He has lectured in Africa and held several visiting professorships in the United States. At present he teaches English and American literature at the University of Glasgow. He is a member of the literature committee of the Scottish Arts Council. He has written critical articles, short fiction, and is author of *Robert Penn Warren: A Vision Earned* (1979).

The first 100 titles

CHINUA ACHEBE	*Arrow of God* *Things Fall Apart*
JANE AUSTEN	*Northanger Abbey* *Pride and Prejudice* *Sense and Sensibility*
ROBERT BOLT	*A Man For All Seasons*
CHARLOTTE BRONTË	*Jane Eyre*
EMILY BRONTË	*Wuthering Heights*
ALBERT CAMUS	*L'Etranger (The Outsider)*
GEOFFREY CHAUCER	*Prologue to the Canterbury Tales* *The Franklin's Tale* *The Knight's Tale* *The Nun's Priest's Tale* *The Pardoner's Tale*
SIR ARTHUR CONAN DOYLE	*The Hound of the Baskervilles*
JOSEPH CONRAD	*Nostromo*
DANIEL DEFOE	*Robinson Crusoe*
CHARLES DICKENS	*David Copperfield* *Great Expectations*
GEORGE ELIOT	*Adam Bede* *Silas Marner* *The Mill on the Floss*
T.S. ELIOT	*The Waste Land*
WILLIAM FAULKNER	*As I Lay Dying*
F. SCOTT FITZGERALD	*The Great Gatsby*
E.M. FORSTER	*A Passage to India*
ATHOL FUGARD	*Selected Plays*

MRS GASKELL	*North and South*
WILLIAM GOLDING	*Lord of the Flies*
OLIVER GOLDSMITH	*The Vicar of Wakefield*
THOMAS HARDY	*Jude the Obscure* *Tess of the D'Urbervilles* *The Mayor of Casterbridge* *The Return of the Native* *The Trumpet Major*
L.P. HARTLEY	*The Go-Between*
ERNEST HEMINGWAY	*For Whom the Bell Tolls* *The Old Man and the Sea*
ANTHONY HOPE	*The Prisoner of Zenda*
RICHARD HUGHES	*A High Wind in Jamaica*
THOMAS HUGHES	*Tom Brown's Schooldays*
HENRIK IBSEN	*A Doll's House*
HENRY JAMES	*The Turn of the Screw*
BEN JONSON	*The Alchemist* *Volpone*
D.H. LAWRENCE	*Sons and Lovers* *The Rainbow*
HARPER LEE	*To Kill a Mocking-Bird*
SOMERSET MAUGHAM	*Selected Short Stories*
HERMAN MELVILLE	*Billy Budd* *Moby Dick*
ARTHUR MILLER	*Death of a Salesman* *The Crucible*
JOHN MILTON	*Paradise Lost I & II*
SEAN O'CASEY	*Juno and the Paycock*
GEORGE ORWELL	*Animal Farm* *Nineteen Eighty-four*
JOHN OSBORNE	*Look Back in Anger*
HAROLD PINTER	*The Birthday Party*
J.D. SALINGER	*The Catcher in the Rye*

SIR WALTER SCOTT

Ivanhoe
Quentin Durward

WILLIAM SHAKESPEARE

A Midsummer Night's Dream
Antony and Cleopatra
Coriolanus
Cymbeline
Hamlet
Henry IV Part I
Henry V
Julius Caesar
King Lear
Macbeth
Measure for Measure
Othello
Richard II
Romeo and Juliet
The Merchant of Venice
The Tempest
The Winter's Tale
Troilus and Cressida
Twelfth Night

GEORGE BERNARD SHAW

Androcles and the Lion
Arms and the Man
Caesar and Cleopatra
Pygmalion

RICHARD BRINSLEY SHERIDAN

The School for Scandal

JOHN STEINBECK

Of Mice and Men
The Grapes of Wrath
The Pearl

ROBERT LOUIS STEVENSON

Kidnapped
Treasure Island

JONATHAN SWIFT

Gulliver's Travels

W.M. THACKERAY

Vanity Fair

MARK TWAIN

Huckleberry Finn
Tom Sawyer

VOLTAIRE

Candide

H.G. WELLS

The History of Mr Polly
The Invisible Man
The War of the Worlds

OSCAR WILDE

The Importance of Being Earnest